THE FURY
OF
BLACKY JAGUAR

ADVANCED PRAISE
THE FURY OF BLACKY JAGUAR
BY ANGEL LUIS COLÓN

"Angel Colón's writing mixes brutal violence with dark humor, but he never forgets the emotional truth of his characters. Colon and THE FURY OF BLACKY JAGUAR should be on everyone's radar now. Readers are going to love this exciting new voice."
— Dave White, Shamus Award Nominated author of NOT EVEN PAST

"THE FURY OF BLACKY JAGUAR is a hardboiled Guy Ritchie-esque romp that clocks you in the jaw and leaves you eager for more the instant the credits roll. Angel Colón is only beginning what is sure to be a career to watch."
— Christopher Irvin, author of BURN CARD and FEDERALES

"I want a Black Jaguar TV series. And an action figure. And a lunch-box. And Blacky-branded brass knuckles. Until that day, I'll settle for this razor-sharp, rattling buzzsaw of a novella."
— Rob Hart, author of NEW YORKED and City of Roses

"Don't let the Heavenly name fool you, Angel Colon's writing brings the heat. THE FURY OF BLACKY JAGUAR is a darkly wry, bare-knuckle brawl of a book that'll leave you seeing stars. Five star reviews that is. I sure as Hell hope Angel has more in store for Blacky Jaguar, because this character has more fight in him than can be contained in a single novella."
— Bracken MacLeod, author of STRANDED and COME TO DUST

ALSO BY
Angel Luis Colón

Hell Chose Me

Pull and Pray

No Happy Endings

Blacky Jaguar Against the Cool Clux Cult

Infested

ANGEL LUIS COLÓN

THE FURY OF BLACKY JAGUAR

A NOVELLA

for Jeanette & Marc

THE FURY OF
BLACKY JAGUAR

'Slainte bradán bod mór agus bás in Eireann'
– A Celtic toast

BLACKY JAGUAR FOUND FRANK VASQUEZ over at his dirty auto garage in Staten Island.

The place had a faded sign that read 'A&J Body Shop' in big, red letters. Blacky wagered it was a hand-me-down business name. Frank was exactly the type to be cheap or lazy enough to keep the original signage. The driveway leading to the garage was old concrete stained with the fluids of all the cars the joint had serviced through the years. Blacky wondered whether customers left their marks driving in or out—he figured the latter. He always thought Frank was a shit mechanic.

Frank was knee deep into a sales pitch for a replacement radiator filter on a brand spanking new Hyundai Elantra—of course, it wasn't needed. The place barely fit the two cars already parked inside. Another mechanic emerged from the single bathroom with a dirty toilet and a repurposed outdoor spigot under a second-hand sink. The entire garage immediately stank to high hell. The customer stood still—nodded at all the right parts of Frank's spiel, but it was obvious she was more concerned with keeping her lunch down.

Blacky was mad—mad that he had to drive here in a Tercel, mad that Frank had the balls to even be in the tri-state, and mad that of all the places he had to be in the entirety of the five boroughs, it had to be Staten Island. His face was flush and he bared his teeth like a junkyard dog as he approached Frank and his client.

"Where the fuck is she?" Blacky's Irish brogue echoed as he walked into the garage. He stepped between Frank and the client. Grabbed Frank's head with both hands and drove it into the Elantra's hood with enough force to take both men off their feet. Blacky scrambled off his knees like a man possessed. Shoved the Elantra's owner to the side and assisted Frank back up to his feet. Brought Frank's head down against the hood a second time. A Pollack splatter of red burst all over the shiny, champagne finish. "Asked a fucking question." Blacky let Frank stay down this time. Paced back and forth with the ease of his namesake.

Frank muttered a string of gibberish words. Spit a wad of bloody phlegm on the floor. Held his face with one hand and reached out for support with the other.

Took three or four attempts before he found the front bumper of a Toyota Corolla. It was late 90's model. Covered in rusted spots, no hood, and hollow on the inside. Frank held himself up against the bumper, still on his knees. Blood dripped onto his shirt in a hurried staccato. He leaned his head back and wiped his face with a groan.

Blacky bent at the waist. He cocked his pompadoured head to the side. "No answer yet?" He produced a custom Sig Sauer P229 from his waist band. An ornately customized piece—hard chrome barrel and a pearl grip. There was ebony lettering on the left side of the barrel that said 'Blacky'. On the right, the letters spelled out, 'Jaguar'. The grip sported an image of said big cat—clinging to the gun and drawing blood. Blacky unlatched the safety, held a finger shy of slipping through the trigger guard. "Seen you eyeing her all the god damn time and now she's gone." He pressed the barrel of the gun against Frank's left cheek. "Where the fuck is she?"

Frank held a hand up. Lost his balance and fell on his ass. "Hold up…hold up…." He was bleeding from both nostrils. His upper lip was split wide open. Front teeth were visible even though his mouth was closed. He staggered to his feet. Braced his weight against a dirty, metal table. Spit again. He still kept a hand up—eyes darted back and forth from the worktable to Blacky. "Be easy…" Frank reached over and snatched a wrench—tried bringing it down at an overhead arc with an overdramatic roar.

Blacky took a single step back. Frank stumbled over himself—whiffed the shot. Blacky watched him wind up for another try. He was tired of this bullshit, so he shot Frank in the leg—right calf, the meaty bit.

Frank dropped to the floor. Let go of the wrench and pawed at his calf with soot-stained hands. "Oh fuck…oh Jesus."

Blacky looked down on him. "Gonna ask again. Where's Polly?"

"Fuck you, stupid mick." Frank sniffed blood and snot back into his nose. Turned his head and coughed a fresh wad back out. "Someone call the fucking cops."

Blacky looked around the garage. Only the Elantra owner—now seated in her vehicle—and another mechanic was present. The other mechanic busy rambling in Spanish. Blacky aimed his gun at him. "Tienes tus papeles?" His Spanish was horrible.

The mechanic's response was to sprint out of the garage—wide-eyed and a prayer pouring from his mouth.

Blacky grinned. Walked over to the Elantra and tapped on the driver's side window with the business end of his gun. "Love, I hope you're not dialing the authorities on that little phone of yours." He eyed a small tribal tattoo at the base of her neck.

The driver held an iPhone to her ear. Slowly lowered

it and gave Blacky a shake of her blonde head. She forced a smile. Any other day and Blacky would have found himself feeding her a few lines—today was not a day for love, though. It was violence all the way for Blacky.

He smiled back. His teeth were dazzling white—all straightened. Blacky was proud of that smile. "Smashing." He motioned towards the open garage exit. "See yourself off. This man and I have a lot to discuss." He walked around to the front of the car. Pulled his own mobile device from his pocket and took a picture of the license plate, then a picture of the owner. Looked to her. "I can find out where you live, so be easy on the squealing, eh?"

Slack jawed terror was all she gave him in response. She started the car.

Blacky stepped to the side and motioned the way a maître d' would to an important customer. The Elantra sped off. The rear scraping the curb as it pulled out onto the main road. A small shower of sparks followed it a few feet before the car disappeared from frame.

Blacky lowered the garage door. Let it come down with a crash. Latched the safety on the Sig and holstered it. Turned on the interior lights, fished a cigarette from the front pocket of his leather jacket, and lit it with a Zippo. The same jaguar that decorated his gun was painted on his lighter. He wandered over to a small mirror hanging over a desk—its frame covered with pictures of Latina centerfolds—all smiles and Hershey kiss nipples. Blacky examined himself for any blood or scrapes—tamed a few out of place hairs and let them settle back into his platinum pompadour. Picked at his teeth. Satisfied with the state he was in; he dragged a chair near Frank and popped a squat. "Looking a little haggard there." He scratched at a thick mutton chop sideburn on the left side of his face. "Nothing to worry about. Made sure it was a flesh wound."

Frank crawled backwards with his hands. Planted his back against the wall and panted. "You're fucking crazy."

Blacky rolled his eyes. Smoothed out a few wrinkles on his chinos. "While my current mental state does correlate to this situation, Francis—it's Francis, right? Well, see, maybe I can be more accommodating if I get what I want." He leaned forward. "One last time— where's Polly?"

Frank sighed. "Fucking bullet in me. This bullshit ain't worth it." He raised a hand. Motioned to Blacky. "Can I get a cigarette?" He frowned. Held the hand out palm up.

Blacky narrowed his eyes. Blew a cloud of smoke straight at Frank. "You're having a fucking laugh?" Took another drag. Jabbed a finger in his direction. "The next fucking bullet's gonna find your bollocks— then it's 'bye-bye cock." He waved to Frank's crotch.

"Shit." Frank slammed his head back against the

wall a few times. Looked to the closed garage door. Moaned. "El Osito." Shifted his weight. "El Osito did it."

The cigarette dangled between Blacky's lips. Bounced in time with his words. "What the fuck are you telling me? Speak English."

"Osito, man. He got Polly." Frank wiped a layer of sweat from his forehead. "Said he'd cut me in on profits—said it was a sure thing. He's got dudes already lined up to take a crack at her."

Blacky hunched over. Crossed his arms and watched the floor. Dragged the heel of a motorcycle boot across an oil stain running from wall to wall. "And where does this Osito fella hang his hat?"

Frank adjusted his legs. Winced. Left a small puddle of blood behind when he bent a knee and brought it to his chest. "Bronx—where else?" He inspected his wound.

Blacky pointed at Frank's bullet wound with his gun. "Imagine if I meant it to be worse." He snapped his fingers between Frank's eyes. "Now, focus. Where in the Bronx?"

He shrugged. "Hunts Point. They got a shop there— Manny's Customs. Only open at night. That's where he does all his side business."

"I should shoot you again for making me come out to Staten Island." Blacky stood up. Slipped his jacket off. Rolled up the sleeves of his wrinkled dress shirt.

It was unbuttoned. A tattoo of Bettie Page draped his midsection. She was holding the sacred heart of Jesus. Underneath his navel, the word 'Rebel' written in Garamond type face. "Still gotta fuck you up."

Frank eyed him and tried to shift his body away from Blacky. "You already shot me." Reached for his wrench.

Blacky kicked the wrench across the dirty floor. "It's a matter of principle." He rolled his neck from left to right. Inhaled and the cherry of the cigarette between his lips brightened. "Can't have you walking around, letting folks know I'm some kind of twatting chump."

"I can't fucking walk." Frank wiped his nose clean—a fat glob of gore stuck to his palm. "I can barely fucking breathe—you mick motherfucker."

"Not enough." Blacky bounded over and delivered a swift kick to the gaping red hole in Frank's calf. Frank screamed, rolled onto his side—tried to fend Blacky off. No use. Blacky brought down a downpour of hammer punches. No rhyme or reason to their destinations. Blacky didn't care *where* they hit. Only mattered that he left his mark. Each hit forced a snowfall of ash from his cigarette. Then the screaming stopped. Frank snored—loud. Blacky cackled. Stood straight and gave Frank another kick to the gut as a parting shot. He collected his jacket. Slung it over his shoulder. Retrieved his phone and connected to 9-1-1.

"Yah? Emergency? Got a guy needs an ambulance."

Blacky let his cigarette fall to the floor. Ground it out under his boot. "Dunno—took a right beating, he did. Needs medical assistance and all that." He smirked at the unconscious Frank.

02

SPECIAL AGENT IRIS DELGADO poked her head into Special Agent Linda Chen's "office"—a converted maintenance closet in the Queens Satellite FBI office. "Chen—got a minute?" The tight bun Delgado kept her hair in bobbed and leaned to the left—made her look as if she'd just walked out of bed.

Linda frowned. She was fiddling with her iPhone. A collection of specialized screws and tools littered her tiny desk. The back of the phone was opened, the battery and micro-SIM to her right. "I'm stuck here, so yes." She searched for a small screwdriver. Checked to see if it rolled off her desk again. Behind her was an 'I want to believe' poster someone superglued to the wall in a tone-deaf attempt to bust her balls. The rest of the space was bare. There was a vent above them meant to spit out air conditioning, but Chen was pretty sure it hadn't performed that function since the late 90's.

"Another crap phone?" Delgado leaned against the door frame.

Chen sighed. "Yeah. Piece of garbage." She closed one eye trying to read microscopic print written on the side of one of the phone's components. "I miss the old flip phones."

"You try to ask for a new one?" Delgado watched her with a small smile. "Or maybe see if there are any spares with the IT guys?"

"That's cute." Chen looked up from her work. "Because anybody here is ready to do me any favors." She rolled her eyes. 'Especially McAllister. Last time I walked by him, I expected him to take me by the throat the way he looked at me." Chen wasn't on good terms with the supervising agent of her group. It was mostly her fault—she didn't deny that.

Delgado shrugged. "It's been two months since the last time you pissed him off."

"Only because I've been living in this closet." She peeked over Delgado's shoulder. "Are you going to come in or is this a public conversation?"

Delgado shook her head. "Nuh uh. This room's hot enough as is. Gets like, ten degrees hotter when there's more than one person in here." She smirked. "And no offense, but you get a little ripe this late in day."

Chen gave her the finger. Went back to her phone. "What's up?"

"Not much. Waiting for my day to end. I was hanging out with the counter-terrorism boys. They got an interesting call." Delgado tucked her thumbs under her belt.

Chen sneered. "Fuck those assholes. Bullshit boys' club they got going. Surprised they haven't built a tree house out front with a wooden sign that say 'no girls.'"

"They got a hit on Clarke." Delgado crossed her arms and leaned in as she said the words.

Chen froze. Slowly lifted her head. "I'm sorry?" She blinked once—twice. She felt her heart rate quicken and her mouth go dry.

Delgado smiled wide—nicotine stained teeth exposed for the entire world to see. "Clarke," she whispered, "They got a hit on Danny Clarke."

Chen motioned for her to close the door.

Delgado rolled her eyes. Stepped into the office and closed the door. Kept her back close to the wall. "Better?"

Chen stood up. Awkwardly walked around her desk. "When did they get the call?"

"Ten minutes ago. He roughed up some mechanic in Staten Island pretty bad."

Chen looked to the side. Took a single step towards a pile of files on a portable radiator. She thumbed through a few folders. "He attacked someone in public?

In Staten Island?" Found the file she was looking for. "Clarke's been inactive for two years and he pops up with aggravated assault?"

Delgado shrugged. "Well, more like attempted murder."

"No explosions?" Chen bit her lower lip. She really hoped he didn't blow anything up again.

Delgado shook her head. "Nope. Are explosions the norm with him?"

Chen ignored the question. "Did he have any prior connection with this mechanic?" Having to interrogate her own partner annoyed the hell out of Chen. She was pretty sure this is why Delgado did it.

Delgado shook her head again. "Nothing obvious."

Chen tossed the folder onto her desk. "That doesn't make sense." She looked back to Delgado. "You know this is off my plate. It's not like I'll be assigned to this."

"It's more of a warning."

"Warning? Why a warning?"

Delgado cracked the door open. Looked up the hall. Turned back and closed the door again. "They want everything you got on him." She pointed at Chen's files. "It's political now. A few folks in office think they can angle this snag as a way to get their asses up the ladder with minimal effort."

"Bullshit." Chen balled her fists. 'That Irish psycho is not minimal effort—I should know that better than anybody else at this office."

Delgado motioned for Chen to lower her voice. "Easy—bring it down. You don't have to tell me about it. Everyone knows you two have history. That's probably why they want your ass completely out of it."

Chen sat back down. "This is such bullshit." She pounded a fist against the desk. A few of her tools rolled off. "All that fucking time spent on this son of a bitch." She bent down to collect the bits and pieces that had scattered on the floor. Chen placed everything on the table and put her phone back together. "The work I did in the field alone."

Delgado watched her. "That's my point—weird history or not, you deserve to catch him."

"Nothing I can do." Chen slipped the battery and the micro-SIM back into their housing slots. Joined the back piece of the phone to the front and worked at keeping them together. "I'll have to give them my files." Switched the phone on—nothing appeared on the screen, but it did beep—it never did that before. She threw her arms into the air. "Fuck it—let them get him."

Delgado arched a brow. "He's your white whale. You're really gonna let Blacky Jaguar go just like that?" She snapped her fingers to accentuate the point.

Chen's face blotched red around the cheeks. She rested her elbows on the top of her plywood desk. "Stop saying that stupid nickname. You realize he made that up, right? Nobody gave it to him."

"And you would know." Delgado slipped her hands into her pants pockets. "You know—I'm supposed to head out and question that mechanic." She smiled. "I might need someone to take notes."

Chen stood up—grabbed her coat and purse. "Fuck you, let's go."

As they walked out of her 'office', Chen turned around. Collected her files and stacked them on her desk. Snatched a Post-it from a drawer and scribbled a note on it. Applied the note to the top of the files. It read: 'HERE YOU GO, FUCK OFF – L. CHEN'. "They can have them. Have most of this shit memorized." She tossed her pen onto her computer keyboard.

Delgado nodded. "Think you'll figure out a way to get him this time?" She walked out into the hallway. Fanned her sweating face.

Chen followed Delgado out. "If he's mixing it up this openly, someone else may get to him first. A man like Blacky Jaguar goes on a rampage; he leaves behind more than a few breadcrumbs to follow."

Delgado turned around. "I meant without it getting personal."

Chen nodded. "He's the one with the hard feelings, Iris." She waved a hand in dismissal. "Besides, I'm only going to help with the interrogation. You guys can do the rest. I don't need to get into any more trouble."

They walked side by side. Delgado laughed to

herself. "You know; you saying that makes me feel like today's going to be real interesting."

03

BLACKY WANDERED INTO GRUMO'S Italian Deli with a big-dick swagger and a smile. One of the last of its kind, Grumo's serviced the fine residents in the Pelham Bay area of the Bronx. There was a large 'For Sale' sign in the front window where oversized replicas of cured meats and cheeses were once displayed. Blacky tried to ignore the sign—he was here for business matters and didn't need to make things more awkward than they were about to get.

Bruno, the owner, was behind the deli counter slicing up a quarter pound of salami. Above him, a board with scattered letters and numbers did little to help anyone know what product was available or how much it would cost them. Grumo's was a local deli—outsiders were damned to guess at what they wanted or needed. Only the regulars were privy to the product and the cost. Bruno preferred it this way—kept things easy for him.

"This fucking guy," Bruno muttered under his breath when he caught sight of Blacky and wiped his hands on his stained apron. A new layer of grease was added to a legacy of cured-meat and cheese stains.

"Bruno, you're looking lovely these days. Lost some weight?" Blacky queued up behind an elderly woman supporting herself on her shopping cart. "I'm fucking famished—what's on deck today?" He eyed the old lady. Crossed his arms and cracked his neck.

The old woman moved a few feet away to wait by the register. Turned her head a few times to make sure Blacky hadn't moved any closer. There was a permanent sneer on her wrinkled face. Her makeup was applied thick—lipstick was too bold and made her lips look crooked.

"Blacky, don't bother my customers." Bruno pointed at an Italian flag curtain separating the main area of Grumo's Deli from the employee-only area. "Anthony's eating lunch in the back. You hurry—you can still have some of the mozzarella on the plate he fixed up for lunch."

Blacky turned. Walked to the row of refrigerators near the back. Ran a finger along the glass, tracking the rows of sodas. "What happened to Royal Crown Draft? You boys stopped carrying it?" He frowned.

All other sodas were shit compared to his beloved RC Draft.

"They stopped making that shit years ago, dummy." Bruno dismissed him. Finished packing up the salami and smiled to his customer. "Un momento." He stomped to the fridges—grabbed Blacky by the collar and shoved him towards the Italian flag curtain. "Go before someone outside sees you."

"Fucking hell, Brunie." Blacky brought his arms up. "Be a little more cordial. How long has it been?" He half lifted the Italian flag. Turned and saw Tony's fat back to him—shoulders hunched over as he dug into his lunch. A TV overhead was showing a soccer match from the Milan Derby.

Bruno ran a hand over his face. "Not long enough." He jabbed a thumb towards the back. "Get moving."

"Alright—fine." Blacky slid the refrigerator door closest to him open and snatched a Manhattan Special. Popped the bottle open and took a swig. Wiped his mouth clean and frowned. "I made a terrible decision with this one." He stared at the bottle with its logo of a 1920's era couple and a cup of espresso. "My god this is shite. How can you sell this in good conscience?"

Bruno waved him off and went back to serving his customer. "Fuck off already."

Blacky laughed and wandered into the back. "Oi, fat ass." He slapped Tony on the back as hard as he could. Placed the bottle of Manhattan Special on the desk next to Tony. "Brought you a gift."

"Fucking Blacky Jaguar," Tony said with a full mouth. He wiped his face and hands off with the bottom of his apron and stood up. Offered Blacky a bear paw of a hand. "And you can keep that vile shit away from me. We only carry it for the older wise guys still running around the neighborhood." He leaned in. "All of them nearly had fits when word got out they stopped distributing it a few years back."

Blacky batted Tony's hand away and gave him a hug. "Fuck the soda, you fat guinea twat. How're yah?" He patted Tony on the back.

Tony hugged him back. "Eh, good as I can be—yah dirty fucking mick." He chuckled. "What's got you out in the wild?"

"Had no intention of poking my head up at all. Been living it up bouncing from mechanic gig to mechanic gig out in Yonkers." Blacky broke the hug. Backed up a few feet and found a seat. "Unfortunately, someone snatched Polly overnight." He let the revelation hang in the air.

Tony's jaw went slack. He sat back down. Swiveled his chair to face Blacky. "Fucking shit, brother. I'm sorry to hear that. What can I do?"

Blacky nodded. Reached over and gave him a pat on the leg. "Thanks. Looking for info on a fella goes by 'Osito.'"

"Osito?"

"Yeah, I think it's Spanish for little bear—maybe."

Tony nodded. "That sounds about right." He scratched his face—got his unshaven chins jiggling. "Any idea where he runs?"

"My contact said he's Bronx local." Blacky snatched at a piece of fresh mozzarella slathered in balsamic vinegar from Tony's plate. He jammed the fresh cheese into his mouth. "I doubt he's this far north, though."

Tony turned his back. Reached into a duffle bag and fished out a laptop. Flipped it open. "This 'contact' still in one piece?" He smirked.

Blacky shrugged. "For the most part…maybe a little brain damage. Might have a limp. Does it matter?"

Tony snorted. "Blacky Jaguar and permanent injuries—ain't much separating the two, huh?"

Blacky laughed. Leaned back and placed his hands behind his head. "Ah, well…" He cocked his head to the side and snickered. "I got nothing." The chair's front legs lifted from the ground and he balanced for a moment before leaning forward.

Tony typed in silence.

"Anything yet?" Blacky stood up. Watched a little bit of the soccer on TV. "How the fuck did you two manage to get real footie on the teevee?" He slipped his leather jacket off. Tossed it on his chair. Dropped to the ground and started doing push-ups.

Tony side-eyed him. "Eh, we still got that dish on

the roof." He typed a little while longer. "Think I got your guy."

Blacky stopped and looked over. "Go on, then. Tell me a story about the little bear." Continued his push-ups.

"Typical bullshit. Three all-expense paid trips Riker's—laundry list of bullshit misdemeanors." Tony's fingers pecked at a cheap keyboard. He reached over and grabbed the Manhattan Special. Drained the bottle in a single pull and frowned after swallowing. "His real name is Hector Ascencio. Says here he ran with the Latin Kings, but I'm not sure if that's still the case."

Blacky counted off, "Thirty-seven, Thirty-eight… why's that? Thirty-nine…" He paused a moment, caught his breath, and started up again.

Tony smirked. "Nobody's writing books on this guy, but I can only assume when one of the biggest gangs in the area breaks away from a guy without burying him, he's knee deep into crazy shit. Maybe he's got juice from something—or someone—else?"

"Good point…forty-five…always had a good head on those shoulders of yours, Tony. Forty-six…." He stopped at the peak of a rep. "Anything else?"

"Other than that, says he's working out of Manny's Customs. Sees his pee-oh regularly. No issues in the last eight months." Tony pawed at a slice of cappricola and shoved it into his mouth. "Whatever he's got going, he's not dumb enough to make it obvious." Tony turned and leaned back in his chair. "Hey man, I'm cool with giving you info, but that's about it this time. Personally, I say you call the cops. I can do it for you, if you want. We can keep it discreet."

"Fifty." Blacky jumped back up to his feet. Stretched his arms out. "Fuck discreet. The boy needs a proper beating—no other way to handle it."

Tony nodded. "I get that. You've got a personal stake. Still, I know you too well, Blacky." He played with the edge of his apron. "You have a habit of lighting dynamite without worrying much about what gets damaged."

"Bullshit." Blacky paced the room. Lit a cigarette. Crossed his arms and stared at a poster for canned anchovies. "Any troubles are on the heads of those willing to cause them."

"But you're the one who stirs the most shit." Tony looked around the room and leaned back to check the Italian flag curtain separating them from the main deli area. "The feds have to know you're stateside now— that fucking mess in Brooklyn a few years ago did you no favors. I can't imagine you got the info on Manny's via a quick and polite phone call."

Blacky sat down and nodded. Stared at a poster for Italian cookies. "Ain't my fault," he muttered. He leaned his neck to the right until it gave a little pop.

"I ain't gonna argue with you." Tony typed. Across the room, a printer came to life. "I already said it: I'll give you what you need, but that's it." He stood—with effort—and waddled over to the printer. Handed Blacky a map from Grumo's over to Manny's Customs. "You're on your own after this."

"I get it." He snatched the paper and frowned. "Didn't mean for all that shit to…"

Tony raised a hand. "We're good. I can't get myself wrapped up in any further adventures is all. No hard feelings."

"Very well." Blacky walked out of the back room. "Be easy, Tony," he called over his shoulder. He gave Bruno a half-hearted wave. "You take care, big man."

Bruno gave him a curt nod. "You too, Blacky."

04

THE EMERGENCY ROOM of Staten Island University Hospital was a madhouse, but Chen willfully ignored the chaos around her. She left Delgado to perform all the niceties—the check-in with administration and the bullshit protocol. They didn't have time. As soon as head office got the word she was out here grilling a victim of this month's hot target, she'd be pulled out by the scruff of her neck. She saw Anchorage, Alaska in her future. Tried not to let that bother her—she had plenty of coats.

She found Frank Vasquez in the Emergency Treatment area. He was a bloodied train-wreck. His nose bandaged. Leg elevated and gauzed. The rest of him seemed absurdly puffy. Chen knew that was all Blacky—he had done a hell of a number on the guy.

Chen lifted his chart and pretended as if she knew what anything scribbled on the form meant. There wasn't any reason besides nosiness to look in the first place.

Frank bleated like a wounded goat. Shifted in the bed slow—careful to not disturb any of his wounds.

Chen put the chart back in its place. "Frank Vasquez?" She inspected his wounds; held her badge up lazily with one hand while she drew the privacy curtain around him with the other.

He nodded.

"Special Agent Linda Chen." She slipped the badge back into her pants pocket. Inspected Frank's wounds—no rhyme or reason to the bumps, bruises, and gashes. It was classic Blacky. "I see you've met someone I'm looking for." She dragged a chair over and sat facing him.

Frank's eyes were glazed over. Chen eyed a line running from his forearm and up to the IV stand. There were two bags of fluid. One was probably pain killers considering the state of him. She wondered how many times he jammed his thumb against the big red button that fed him his allotment of momentary relief. In Chen's opinion, this schmuck got off lucky. She knew the kind of damage Blacky could do—she'd seen it.

Chen snapped her fingers in front of Frank's face. "You home?"

Frank winced and frowned. "I got shot." He

continued with his fidgeting—tried to make himself comfortable on the uncomfortable looking bed.

"I can see that." Chen crossed her legs. Leaned in. "Look, I'm in a hurry, so I apologize for my bedside manner—but I don't give a fuck if he cut your cock off and shoved it up your fat ass." She smiled. "I want to know where you sent him."

He stared at her moment. It was obvious he was weighing his options. "I don't know shit," he slurred.

Chen sighed. Stood up and unholstered her Glock. She slammed the bottom of its grip against the bandages on Frank's calf as hard as she could. With the painkillers, a little extra effort would be needed so she did it twice. When she saw the pain begin to register on his face she leaned over and covered his mouth with a hand. Pressed the business end of her sidearm against his temple.

"That's really going to hurt in a few seconds—much worse than now." She grinned. "Now, when I move my hand you get—at most—five words. If I don't know where Blacky Jaguar is before those five words, your legs are going to have matching holes. Am I clear?"

Frank's eyes widened. A near whispered 'yes' slipped from between his teeth.

"Wonderful." She moved her hand. Repositioned the gun to his left calf. "Tell me what I want to know."

Frank sniffed. "Manny's Customs, Hunts Point."

Chen holstered her gun. "Bonus points for word

economy, Frank." She sat back down. "Now what's got Blacky beating the hell out of you and then headed over to The Bronx to cause more problems?"

"We took her. Motherfucker went crazy…shit. I woulda given him a cut." Frank looked away. Grit his teeth as his pain receptors caught up with the action. "Fuck." He jabbed at a red button at his side repeatedly. Nothing happened—he'd had his fill of pain meds for the hour.

Chen arched a brow. "Took who?"

Frank ignored her. Reached up to inspect his IV bags.

Chen kicked the corner of his bed. "Come on, Frank, focus for me. Who did you guys take?"

"What?" He seemed to almost deflate. "All of ya'll are fucking crazy, you know that?" Now he was whining.

"I'll ask again. What did you people steal from Blacky Jaguar that would get him to poke his head out of the ground after two fucking years?" Chen raised a foot to kick the bed again.

Frank's eyes lit up. "Oh, yeah. See…there was money to be made. So we took her. We took Polly. Osito said he'd get top fucking dollar…" He trailed off.

"Polly?" Chen thought back on Blacky's background. Daniel Clarke (potentially an alias), worked out of Northern Ireland in the 90's for the IRA. He came to the States before 9/11. Ran around doing oddjobs for the occasional criminal douchebag.

Nothing as major as what he pulled in Ireland, but it was enough—kidnapping, racketeering, murder. Blacky wasn't very picky about his gigs. He had quite a few known associates; the Rafe sisters, the IRA's own Thomas Curren (believed dead), Aleksei Uryvich out in Coney Island—no Polly, though.

"Yeah man, Polly's gonna move some cash once they get her to the right people." Frank looked away. His eyelids drooped.

"Chen?" Delgado pulled the privacy curtain aside and walked into the area. "Is this our man?" She seemed unimpressed.

Chen nodded. "Yeah, he says Blacky's causing mischief on account of a 'Polly' being taken from him." She narrowed her eyes. "That can't be a drug, right?"

Delgado shook her head. "You're thinking of Molly."

Frank snored.

"Alright, so it's not drugs. Blacky's no saint, but he's never played in that sandbox before." Chen scratched the back her neck.

"Maybe a girlfriend?" Delgado crossed her arms. Leaned her head to the side.

"No, he's not one for commitments." She frowned. "Knowing him—it's something incredibly stupid. Something only *he* would get irrationally mad about." She walked herself through the last few hours. Blacky attacked Frank in his garage because Polly was missing and he wanted to know where she was. Frank was shot and assaulted—gave Blacky an address in Hunts Point for a place called 'Manny's Customs'. Chen blinked. It was obvious. She kicked Frank's bed again. "Frank, come back to us."

Frank smacked his dried lips. His eyes fluttered open. "Hmm?"

"Polly—what's the make and model?"

Delgado made a face like someone farted. "What the hell are you…?"

Chen raised a hand for her to quiet down. "Make and model, Frank."

He took a long breath. Looked at Delgado and gave a weak smile. "'sup?"

Chen gave the bed three more kicks. "He's high as a kite. One last time, Frank; what's the make and model of the car you stole from Blacky Jaguar?"

"Jesus, why you have to cop that bullshit hard ass attitude for?" Frank swallowed. "It's um, what do you call it, a Plymouth Fury…nineteen fifty nine. Sick whip."

Delgado's jaw dropped. "He did this to you over a car?"

Frank went back to sleep.

Chen stood up. "I knew it was something frivolous." She tapped Delgado on the shoulder. "See what you can find out about registrations for that make and model. Has to be a rare one."

Delgado nodded. "And you?"

Chen raised her hands up in mock surrender. "I'm done. I don't need the stress in my life—not over a car." She fished her phone from her pocket. Tried to turn it on. Another beep. "Besides, I should probably go to a store about this bullshit phone."

"Sure." Delgado gave her the side-eye. "So you're done. You're going to let someone else bring Blacky in?"

Chen stared at her phone. "So, I'll see you later, okay?"

Delgado watched Frank sleep. Snapped her head to Chen in realization. "Wait, we came in your car."

"Get a uniform to drive you in. I really need to take care of this." She made a beeline out of the ER. Figured she had an hour—two at best—before they figured out where she was going. Chen wasn't lying about going to the store first, though. If she was going to find Manny's Customs, she'd need a way to find the fucking place. She pocketed the phone and grumbled under her breath. "Fucking stupid technology…"

05

IT WASN'T HARD TO FIND 'Manny's Customs'. Blacky sat on the hood of his 'borrowed' Tercel and cracked his knuckles. He muttered a litany of curses under his breath and lit a cigarette. Decided to take a walk around to the trunk of the car. Popped it open and pulled a cinderblock from inside. Blacky placed it to the side, got into the car, turned it on, and positioned it to face the storefront of the joint where they were holding Polly. He put the car in park and reached around back to procure the Remington 12-guage seated behind him. Picked up the satchel in the passenger's seat loaded with rock salt shells. Cigarette clenched between teeth, he stepped back outside—leaving the driver's side door open—and slipped the satchel over his shoulder. Double-checked the shotgun was loaded.

Blacky ashed his cigarette and slipped it back between thin lips. He grabbed the cinder block, secured it over the gas pedal of the Tercel, and checked to make sure there was no cross traffic. Satisfied, he put the car into drive. The Tercel didn't break any land speed records, but by the time it tore through the front window of Manny's Customs, it had picked up more than enough speed to clear a massive path inside. The poor car collapsed its front against a concrete wall— no big loss. Blacky walked through the new hole and surveyed the damage. Two young men lay sprawled out to his right. Both breathing, but unconscious. To his left—a stunned fat man behind the counter. There were rows of posters with beautiful women draped over beautiful cars—all askew, but unmoved in the black void of their existence. Above them, a neon sign with the store's name flickered a few times and died. Blacky grinned, spit his cigarette out and leveled the Remington as he approached his new friend. "Good fucking evening."

The cashier looked past Blacky and at the carnage in the store. Blacky knocked him on the head with the barrel of his shotgun. "Now mind your manners and answer a person back when they greet you." He aimed the gun between the cashier's eyes single-handed. "Or I could always educate you with a little corporal punishment."

The cashier responded with a string of Spanish curses.

Blacky recognized a few—'cabron' and 'pendejo' were favorites. He sighed. Aimed the Remington at the fattest part of the cashier's arm, stepped back a few paces, and fired.

The shot pushed the cashier against the wall. "Motherfucker!" He turned on a heel—clutched the shredded meat of his shoulder. "Maricon! Hijo de la gran puta!"

Blacky pointed to the barrel of his shotgun with the peak of his pompadour. "Hey now. The homophobia and insults against my dear mother is going to get my finger twitchy again, friend." He leveled the gun back to the cashier's face. "Let's avoid peppering that ugly mug of yours." He flashed a smile. "Now, I'm looking for a fella called Osito, or shit, if Manny himself is around, I'd love to bend his ear too."

"They the same fucking dude," the cashier spoke between his teeth. He leaned against the countertop. His new wounds wept red down his side. Ran down his jeans and onto his boots. "Yo, you coulda just walked in instead of trying to kill everyone."

Blacky smirked. "Nah. Rock salt hurts like a motherfucker, but you'll live." He crooked his head to the side. Frowned. "Well, if you see a doctor at some point." Blacky reached into his back pocket with a free hand. Produced a switchblade, let the business end out, and promptly drove into the cashier's hand on the Formica countertop.

The cashier screamed. Fell to his knees and lashed around like a fish. He tried to pull his hand up, but the switchblade found itself fond of the Formica—wouldn't budge unless true effort was applied.

Blacky watched his prey—patient—cold steel in his eyes. "Compose yourself." He reached into his jacket pocket with a free hand and produced a cigarette. Sent the hand back in for the lighter. He flicked the Zippo open and had it lit in a single motion. Took a long drag to get the cigarette going, let it slowly roll to the right corner of his mouth, then let out a thick cloud of smoke from the opposite side. "So where's your employer?"

The cashier remained on his knees. Looked up at Blacky. "I told you he ain't here." His voice was strained—eyes were wet with tears, drool ran from the corners of his mouth. Made a face like a toddler about to cry from a skinned knee.

"Then what do you know about a '59 Plymouth Fury? Black—convertible. Fully restored with a few bells and whistles." Blacky twitched his lip to force ash off the end of his cigarette. Grey snow gently settled onto the cashier's pinned hand—darkened and shrunk into black dots when in contact with the fresh blood pooling under the cashier's hand.

"Fuck you." The cashier spit at Blacky. Tried to raise his shotgun wounded arm up to get the knife out of his hand. Blacky tapped the knife with the barrel of Remington. Sent the cashier into another spasm. "Fucking shit, man. Please!" His eyes were wild.

Blacky cackled. "Stop twatting around, then. Tell me where I can find Osito and we're good. You can go patch yourself up, maybe even get the hell out of here before the cops show up." He checked his watch. Already five minutes since he crashed the Tercel into the store. This kind of neighborhood—they'd be lucky to hear a siren in another ten minutes.

The cashier slowly rose to his feet. Ranted a little more in Spanish.

Blacky kept the shotgun pressed against the knife. "Where's Osito?"

"Probably at his house on Fteley." The cashier winced. He lowered his gaze to the floor and licked his lips.

Blacky stared at the cashier blankly. Waited a beat for a little more information—preferably one that made more sense than a gibberish word like, 'Fteley'. "You think I have a fucking clue what you're saying? Address, yah daft bastard."

"I look like I can hold a pen right now?" He glared at Blacky. There was a hint of bravery beginning to come out of his clouded eyes.

Blacky grunted. Reached over the counter and grabbed a pen. He tore a slip of receipt paper from the top of the cash register and readied himself to take down the address. "Spill it."

"Fuck you." The cashier sneered. He sniffed snot into his nose and spit on the floor. Puffed his chest out a little.

The courage set off Blacky's alarms. "Damn it."

He turned in time to see top of the shaved head belonging to the idiot about to slide tackle him against the counter. Blacky made an attempt to side step, but it was too late. The brute connected, threw Blacky off guard. Managed to get a hand on the shotgun. Glass shattered. They struggled a moment while Blacky attempted to get his footing. The cashier, though, he mustered up the strength to bring his wounded arm up. He wrapped his hand around the barrel of the shotgun and made it a three-way fight. The chaos—swinging hands, shifting legs—forced Blacky's finger to press against the trigger when the barrel of the shotgun was dangerously close to the cashier's face.

The retort startled Blacky and his attacker. Even with rock salt in those shells, the force of the blast wiped the flesh from the cashier's lower jaw clean off. He crumpled back to his knees and disappeared behind the counter. Only his hand—still pinned to the countertop by Blacky's switchblade—remained in view. The cashier's middle finger twitched for a moment, then went still.

Blacky and his attacker both stood frozen. The

attacker held on to the shotgun—leaned over the counter to check on the cashier. "Yo, you fucking killed him."

"Fuck yourself." Blacky pointed to his attacker with his chin. "If the two of you weren't playing tug of war—everything would be fine."

"Yeah, but you had your finger on the trigger." The attacker stared down at Blacky's hand.

Blacky slipped his finger off the trigger. "Of course, I had my fucking finger—that's how a god damn gun works, yah daft bastard."

"Not if you ain't trying to kill a dude."

"Who's to fucking say I wasn't gonna kill him after the fact?"

"So you were gonna kill him, see? You admitted that shit." The attacker sneered.

"Maybe yes, maybe no. I like to keep my options open." Blacky shrugged. "Still, this wasn't my choice. Not my fault if you forced me to do it." Now he leaned his head over the countertop. "He might still be breathing, you know."

His attacker narrowed his eyes. "Yo, why can't you be a man and own it? Your stupid ass shoulda kept your finger off the trigger."

"Because you forced my fucking hand—literally." Blacky tried to pull away from his attacker. Pivoted his hips and made an attempt to throw a punch. He was interrupted by a second man with the same haircut and uniform as the other. The shotgun was snatched away and its stock smashed against his chin. His vision blurred. The shotgun hit a second time. The world went white.

"Who the fuck is this corny, Elvis looking mother-fucker?" A heavily accented voice boomed from what felt to Blacky to be miles away.

"Yo, he shot Petey in the face. Tried saying it was me and the dude…"

Blacky wanted to argue against the point. Wanted to explain that he hadn't been at fault for giving the cashier a shave with the shotgun. His head went shaking again, but he felt no pain. His head felt underwater—the little light in the store bent and glared.

That was about the time it all went quiet for Blacky Jaguar.

06

CHEN ARRIVED AT MANNY'S CUSTOMS in time to see two men dragging the groggy Irish bastard out of the obliterated storefront. She watched them dump Blacky into the trunk of a Mazda. One had a shotgun in hand and the other was unarmed. They got into the car and seemed to get into an animated discussion. Chen figured they were trying to make sense of the crazy Irishman that drove a car through a storefront instead of knocking like a normal, sane criminal.

"Shit, shit, shit…" She fumbled for her new phone. Selected her contacts and balked—she forgot to import all of her phone numbers. "God damn it." There was no way to get back to home office or Delgado. Sure, they were probably on their way, but with Blacky in the trunk of a car something had to be done now.

Chen sighed. Waited for the Mazda to pull out of the lot and drive off. She shifted her car into drive after a ten count and tailed them from three to four cars behind. "What did you do now, Danny?"

They drove for a few minutes on the local roads and then merged onto the Cross Bronx Expressway. The Mazda took the exit near the Soundview-Morrison section of The Bronx. Chen followed a little closer. The Mazda's driver showed no sign of knowing he was being tailed—she hoped. They didn't drive much longer. Two right turns and they reached their destination. The side of Fteley Avenue they turned onto led to Story Avenue—right next to the Cross Bronx and the Bruckner Expressway. Chen figured these perps must have a lot of traffic to want to live so close to the highway. She kicked herself for not programming Delgado's number into her phone before heading out to Manny's Customs. Knew Delgado was going to bust her balls big time over that one when the time came.

Her target parked in the driveway of a two floor house on Fteley Avenue. It was getting near dark. A few stray kids were playing down the street. Stray adults were skulking around accomplishing nothing more than walking from stoop to stoop. Chen parked her car across the street a few cars ahead and watched. The two thugs who took Blacky got out of the car. The passenger ran up the front stairs of the house and knocked on the door. After a minute, the door opened halfway and he leaned in—his hands moving as he told his story. Whoever he was speaking to closed the door and the passenger yelled down to the driver. The two-car garage in front of them opened up and a young, overweight boy motioned the car to pull into an empty spot right next to a shiny, black Plymouth Fury.

"Oh shit—the Plymouth," Chen said to herself.

The driver got back into the Mazda and pulled the car in while leaving his door ajar. He cut the engine, popped the trunk, and hopped out as the garage door lowered.

Chen bit her lower lip. She could call 911, tell them how she was tracking a suspect—get a fleet of cops over as soon as possible. That would not only save Blacky's ass, but she'd have him. There'd be no way he could slip away this time. Chen rubbed her temples then eyed the house. Knowing Blacky like she did, there'd be no way he would last long—not with a mouth like his. There'd be a bullet in between his eyes before the end of the night.

"Fine…fine…" She checked her sidearm. Checked her phone—no messages or missed calls—of course. Chen stepped out of her car. A few kids ran by her and gave her the stink-eye. She wasn't sure if it was the general sentiment or if anyone in the area was used to seeing a half Chinese half German girl in a terrible pantsuit. The air outside was sticky—humid—felt like she was walking inside a warm bath.

"Yo, what's good, baby?" The voice came from behind her. Sounded like the guy was choking on shards of glass.

Chen felt something cold crawl up her spine. Not even a minute outside of the fucking car. The Bronx wasn't the same animal as the other boroughs. The rest of the city was dirty, but had sheen over it—fake diamonds in an ashtray. The Bronx, as far as she could see, was all ashtray. She walked around the front of her car and crossed the street. Ignored the call. Took care to avoid quickening her pace. No need to act like a deer in the wild.

"Ma, you hear me?" The voice was following her. The volume was increased.

Chen kept walking towards the house. Kept her eyes on the metal bars lining the second floor windows and listened to the salsa music blaring from a ground floor apartment window half a block up. Somewhere, someone was frying chicken. The windows of the house Blacky was taken to were obstructed by black out curtains—strange choice for such a hot day. A single window unit air conditioner hummed from its perch on a main floor window.

"Damn girl, don't be so stuck up." A hand brushed her shoulder.

That did it. She turned, angry. Ready to unleash hell on this fuck-head.

Unfortunately the voice came with a Smith &

Wesson pointed right at her nose. It was attached to a lanky fella. Wild eyed, his face was covered in pockmarks. He wore a Knicks jersey three sizes too large. Track marks up and down his arms—a cartography of self-abuse. "You following my boys?"

Chen tried to keep her jaw set. Couldn't understand how they knew she was tailing them. She took care—made sure they didn't notice.

A car door slammed across the street. A mountain of a man walked over to them. "This the bitch that was following Luis and Marcos?" Big Man was wearing a companion jersey to the druggie. Wore a ring on each knuckle. A watch with a face the size of Chen's fist sat on his thick wrist.

Chen looked down. It wasn't that the guys she tailed noticed her—no—it was the sons of bitches that followed them. She noticed that the neighborhood was suddenly crypt silent..

The lanky guy with the piece grinned. "See? I fucking told you she was following them." He reached forward and brushed a hand from her waist and down between her legs—spent a little longer than he needed at the crotch. He pulled her sidearm, then her wallet. Handed it over to the Big Man.

Big Man opened her wallet and his eyes widened. "Well damn, eff-bee-eye, huh?"

She stayed silent. Took stock of the situation. Only one of them was armed and seemed to be tweaked to the gills. The one with her wallet, while larger, was a bigger target. If Chen moved fast enough—deliberately enough—she would be able to incapacitate both of them, get back to her car, and call for back up. She decided she was an asshole for not doing that first, but opted to have the pity party later.

The Big Man grinned. Read her like a book. "Don't go thinking you got a way out, sweetheart." He jabbed a thumb at the Junkie. "My man's not all here, but I'm damn sure his finger is quicker than your fist."

Junkie licked his lips. Eyes were bugged out like a scared Chihuahua's. "I can cap her right here. Nobody's gonna give a shit about some Chinese bitch walking around the wrong neighborhood getting shot." He lowered the heater, pressed the barrel against Chen's left breast, and smiled—traced the area where she figured he assumed her nipple would be. He was off about a half inch.

Chen frowned. Raised her hands. "Fine." She realized they hadn't taken her phone—tucked neatly into her jacket's inside pocket. With luck, they wouldn't pat her down again. Her badge had given them something else to think about. She nodded—decided to keep her mouth shut. There wasn't a need to make things difficult. Chen said a silent 'thank you' to whoever was above for the stupidity of the average gun thug. Having her phone around could pay off—somehow.

Big Man smiled wide. There were two gold teeth in

his mouth among the many grey and brown capped ones. "At least you're smarter than that other dude. Turn that ass around and get moving then."

Chen did as she was told.

Junkie jabbed his gun hard between her shoulder blades. "Speed it up."

They led her to the garage door that had closed moments ago. Big man pressed a button on his key dongle and the door rose. The hum of the pneumatic a blaring whine. Inside, the Mazda and the Fury sat idle. The Mazda's trunk was open—no Blacky. The garage was near sterile aside from the presence of the cars. The walls were bare and freshly painted. The floors were freshly mopped. Chen noticed that there weren't even spider webs in the dark corners. Made her wonder if that Fury inspired this level of cleanliness or if the home's owner was that OCD.

Her captors led her to the front of the Mazda. Big Man disappeared through a door with a stairway leading up to the main house. There were voices and laughter from inside. A few minutes later, Big Man returned with a chair and an extension cord. The chair was slid over to her. "Sit the fuck down."

Chen sat down. Did them the favor of placing her arms behind her.

"Shit, she's a good girl." Big Man roughly wrapped the extension cord around her wrists. Ran the rest down and under the chair and around her ankles. He tied it off tight. Gave the cord an extra tug to assure that he knew what he was doing.

Chen wore her best poker face—didn't want to clue either of them in on the fact she thought they were morons by rolling her eyes or sneering. Delgado said she had a habit of wearing her judgments on her face. Whether it was true or not, this was Chen's first time as a hostage—better safe than sorry.

Junkie looked back and forth from Big Man to Chen. "Yo, we should shoot her now—less to worry about later." He was anxious—ready for blood.

"Not yet. Osito wants us upstairs with the Elvis dude. Luis and Marco had to handle dinner upstairs." He sucked his teeth and eyed Chen—pointed at her with his chin. "After that, we can have a party with this bitch. Do whatever the fuck we want with her." He took Junkie by the arm and pulled him towards the door leading back into the house.

The Junkie gave a Jack-o'-lantern smile to Chen. Holstered his piece. "Yeah…yeah…I'm bout that."

Chen closed her eyes. Took a long breath. She listened to their footsteps as they walked away and closed the door. When she felt like they were definitely upstairs and she was alone, Chen opened her eyes. She tucked her chin into her chest and made an attempt to loosen the extension cord around her wrists. There was give, but she got a little too enthusiastic. Tipped over on the chair and fell to the floor on her left side.

The floor was cold against her face. Her new phone fell out of her pocket and slid a foot away—taunted her as the screen illuminated, waiting to be unlocked.

She sighed. "Fuck my life."

07

"WAKE UP." A small, rough hand smacked Blacky across the face—hard.

Blacky grit his teeth. Tasted pennies at the back of his throat. His head felt like a balloon—empty and bloated. He blinked and winced. A jolt of pain ran from his eyes down to the roof of his mouth. That much told him his nose was broken. He was seated. Felt two pairs of strong hands holding him at either shoulder. Blacky shook his head. Leaned forward as far as his handlers would allow him and spit on the floor.

"Why you gotta be spitting on my floor, dude? You don't got manners?" The voice was gruff—lightly accented. He said a string of words in Spanish. The sound of people running up stairs came from behind.

Blacky frowned—more than three assholes were in the house. The odds were severely against him today.

Blacky looked up at the etiquette expert. "Wait… what?" He was a little startled at the sight of him.

The owner of the voice stood with muscled arms crossed over his bare chest. The guy was ripped—looked like a super-hero. Shaved head, angry eyes, faded prison tattoos—all on a frame that teased five feet tall. His width almost matched his height. The fella was a bodybuilder, a veined freak of nature. His face still had traces of baby fat at the cheeks. He wore cargo pants that were probably pulled from the juniors section at Target. The Doc Martens on his feet were oversized. Gave him the appearance of a shit-kicking clown. A child-like, shit-kicking, muscle bound clown.

"Is this a fucking joke?" Blacky's voice was hoarse. He coughed and it felt like sand coated the walls of his throat.

The little man smirked. Took a step forward and laid a punch into Blacky's breadbasket with the force of a man twice his size.

Blacky lost his air. He choked and threw his head back—wide-eyed and now more aware then he'd been before.

"You been asking for me, now you got me." A stubby finger floated in front of Blacky's vision.

"Ah, Osito." Blacky coughed again. He nodded. Looked Osito up and down. "Think I get the whole motif too. You got eff-ess-gee-ess. Treatment threw you for a loop, huh?" His lungs burned as his air returned to him. Gut ached something fierce from the punch. That was going to bruise, he knew it.

Osito blinked. "What the fuck you know about that?" He fingered a large, silver cross hung from a thick rope chain around his neck.

Blacky smiled. The blood from his nose had dried above his lip. The dark red mustache cracked around the edges. "Your kidneys are fucked up. You've probably had all sorts of issues. I reckon it hit yah young—the steroids fucked you up—kept you looking like an altar boy. Shame you don't act like one."

Osito nodded slowly. Frowned. "Whatever, yo. Acting like he fucking knows me and shit." He motioned to Blacky's handlers. "Balls on this dude." Osito looked back to Blacky. "You a doctor, you know so much about me?"

Blacky smiled. "Nah, just a big fan of Gary Coleman is all."

His handlers straightened him up. The Big Man gave Blacky a knock to the side of the head with an elbow and sniggered. Blacky made a mental note to do something awful to him once he felt up to snuff. Above them; footfalls. The sound of yelling. Blacky thought he heard a woman's voice cry out. He chalked it up to the cake batter state of his brains.

Osito paced in front of Blacky. Behind him, a full

complement of free weights and benches set at inclines and declines and other angles Blacky had no knowledge of. There was a treadmill in the corner of the room that looked like it belonged in a spaceship, not a shitty three-floor house in the asshole of the Bronx. Blacky weakly pointed over at a row of dumbbells arranged in ascending order of weight from right to left. "You work out?" He had an 'a-ha' moment. "You're still on the fucking 'roids, little fella?"

Osito laughed. "Something like that." He motioned to the Big Man and Junkie. "Get this motherfucker on his feet."

They pulled Blacky to his feet with unnecessary force. His legs were wobbly, but he was able to get his bearings. He felt a small rush of energy hit him—maybe a second wind. Decided to hold off a little longer in case it was a fluke. "I just want my fucking car back." He spit again. Head felt like someone was trying to punch out of it. "You got it right in the garage. Won't be much trouble to give it back. We can put all the ugliness behind us."

"*Your* car?" Osito looked up to Blacky with a smile. "You did all this shit for the Plymouth?" He delivered another punch to Blacky's gut. Stepped back and grunted. "You fucked up my boy Frank and it's sounding a lot like my cousin Pete's not making it through the night."

Blacky's eyes rolled into the back of his head. He

nearly fell face forward, but only went limp for a breath. That second wind was looking like the mother of all flukes. "Cousin?" he managed to squeeze the word out between the spaces where his head didn't throb. "I told that idiot the guy was still breathing."

Osito eyed him. "The car's mine now. The bitch that followed you here is mine too." He reached up and pulled Blacky down by the collar. "And as far as I'm concerned, *you're* mine."

Bitch? Blacky wasn't sure what Osito was blabbing about. Best to ignore and move on, but he certainly didn't need any outside parties getting hurt on account of him. He chortled. "I ain't housebroken—fair warning." Blacky straightened up. Felt another surge, but this time his head felt clear—startlingly so. Had to be adrenaline. Fight or flight was kicking in—he smiled. Leaned his head against the shoulder of Big Man to his right. Studied Junkie opposite him. "Got a bit of a rough streak in me too." He brought his forehead forward as hard as he could against Junkie's nose. The slack-jawed moron staggered back and tripped over his own legs. Took a broken nose dive down the stairwell leading to the basement.

"Maricon!" Big Man pulled at Blacky and caught him with a hard right hook. He brought his fist back to deliver another one—this time with more feeling.

Blacky pushed through the pain, wrapped his hands over Big Man's face, and jammed his thumbs into Big Man's eyes as hard as he could. Blacky felt the gelatin give under his fingertips. He curved them to ensure his fingernails got a little of the action. If he didn't blind the son of a bitch now, an infection would surely finish the job another day. Big Man screamed and kicked Blacky away.

Big Man fell back and held his hands over his eyes. "Jesus Christ, Osito, I think he fucked up my eyes for real." He let out a noise that sounded more like disappointment than pain.

Blacky spit on Big Man. Swung his leg in a wide arc—field goal style—at his head. That shut the Big Man up. Blacky turned to face Osito—sniffed and felt a thick wad of bloodied snot travel down his throat. "Sorry…I got personal space issues."

Osito grinned. Cracked his neck. "Not for long."

Blacky raised a finger. "Quick question before this gets serious."

"What?" Osito spread his feet shoulder width. Eyed Blacky up and down. His eyebrows arched up. It was obvious he enjoyed the drama.

"How much were you getting for my Polly?"

"The car?" Osito scoffed. "Shit, man. You know how many old, white assholes from North Jersey I had knocking on my door as soon as that shit went live?" He sniggered. "Shit, you make an offer right now, I might be down. Though, the VIG is gonna be a bitch."

Blacky nodded. "Wanted to confirm is all. I'll give

you some credit; you do have a fine taste in vehicles." He raised his fists, rolled his shoulders loose. "I'm, unfortunately, low on funds. Unless you count a beating as payment." He grinned. "Wax the floor with you; I get my car back and a story for the pub. Fucking electrifying."

They circled each other—caged animals ready to clash. The AC in the window opposite them struggled to maintain the temperature now that the room saw an increase in testosterone. It hummed loud—desperate to break the silence. Blacky licked the back of his hand and tried to wipe his upper lip clean. Pressed a thumb against his left nostril and shot a snot rocket at the floor.

Osito breathed through his nose. "You about to make my fucking day." He had the grace of a boxer—light on his feet with heavy fists. He had a height disadvantage, but the way he moved made it apparent that it wasn't a worry to him. Osito was fighter—a survivor. Some gangly mick was no obstacle to him.

Blacky almost laughed out loud he was so excited.

A shot rang out and interrupted the festivities. The bullet struck the ceiling—plaster and drywall dropped down and littered one of Osito's weight benches. More than one woman screamed from upstairs. Blacky and Osito turned to the shooter.

"Hands up." Special Agent Iris Delgado stared at

Blacky down the sight of her Glock. "Both of your asses are under arrest."

08

CHEN HEARD SOMEONE TUMBLE down the stairs and hit the door to the basement. She froze—halfway free from the power cord Big Man and Junkie decided to bind her with. After a few beats and no open door, she went back to work. It wasn't difficult to get her hands free, but the knot that bound her legs was a pain in the ass on account of sweaty hands. There seemed to be plenty of time to work on freedom, so she was at least calm enough to deal with a few speed bumps.

She snatched her phone and hurried to her feet. She looked around the garage for something—anything—that she could use as a weapon. The only object in the entire space other than the two cars was a locked storage pantry. The voices upstairs spoke quickly. She wondered if Blacky was already dead. That had to be it—no way was he going to make it out of this. He had to be the one that took the spill down the stairs. She stood between the Plymouth and the Mazda and thought. Blacky was a lunatic—there had to be something in his car.

The Fury's top was down—thankfully—so Chen was able to search it thoroughly. To Blacky's credit; it was a beautiful machine. The top coat—jet black, mirrored—she could see every feature of her face clearly in it. The upholstery was that fancy leather, the kind that almost felt like velvet. Every bit of it was restored to its original glory. She imagined Blacky riding around, listening to Elvis or The Everly Brothers—the latter his secret favorite band. Chen ran a hand over the steering wheel. The car was a piece of art—she could grant Blacky that point. Still, nice car or not, this amount of chaos for a material possession was insanity—she'd never understand why he would go to these lengths.

There was nothing going on in the front or back seat of the Fury beyond what appeared to be a fresh cigarette burn in the passenger seat. Chen winced—felt sorry for whoever did that if Blacky got his hands on them. She moved to the trunk and popped it open. The inside was torn apart. Under the lining there was a small black box; beside it, a large battery. Chen's eyes widened. "That makes sense," she said. It was a LoJack receiver. With a classic car like this, it was a wonder Blacky didn't have a dozen anti-theft deterrents. She checked the box. It wasn't connected to a main power source—only needed the battery. Chen slipped the battery back into the receiver and a green light slowly came to life on top of the unit. She lifted the liner in the trunk and managed to find a faraway spot to jam the receiver into. She unlocked her phone and dialed 911. Gave them the riot act—special agent, taken prisoner, potential violence, LoJack signal for a Plymouth Fury with a South Carolina license plate reading CDI-498.

They told her backup would be incoming. Said to stay out of harm's way. Chen laughed and told the dispatcher they needed to get a move on it—there were no guarantees of her safety. "Don't think the en-why-pee-dee needs a dead special agent in the papers," she said facetiously.

Chen disconnected the call and continued to search Blacky's Fury. She managed to find a tire iron. That was disappointing—useful—but disappointing. She expected to find something capable of exploding or making a fire. With tire iron in hand, she took her scavenging over to the Mazda. There was nothing useful inside of it beyond a pack of Newports with a single cigarette and a set of keys. For a moment, she entertained lighting the cigarette up and indulging in a little stress relief. By her count it had been nearly a decade since she even touched a cigarette—a Lebanese brand called Cedars, if she remembered it right. Chen stared at the pack and shook her head. "Not a good time for a return to bad habits, girl." She crumpled the pack and tossed it over her shoulder—regret made a nest at the pit of her stomach.

She pocketed the keys in case she found herself with her back against the wall—as if that wasn't the case already. But then, she did have a way out. She could open the garage door, make a run for it—even wait for the police to arrive. Chen stared at the basement door then looked to the garage door. She owed Blacky nothing. The time she spent working his case, obsessing over his history—it wasn't worth her life. She let the tire iron slide down her hand a little, ready to let it go.

A gunshot. Chen nearly jumped out of her skin. The drive to leave grew; it ran a stark streak of concentrated cowardice down her back. There'd be no shame in running—she knew that, knew it was probably the more responsible choice. It was a suicide run. A lone, shit-stain of a federal agent running into a gunfight? Chen had her tally of dumb decisions during her tenure as special agent, but even she gave herself the benefit of the doubt—she was no hero.

Which is why it was so weird that she found herself with the tire iron gripped in her right hand and her left hand turning the door knob leading upstairs. Chen slowly opened the door. She peeked through a crack that wasn't more than a quarter inch wide. All she saw was cheap carpet and a piece of the wall directly above. The Junkie was at her feet—eyes closed and arms akimbo. He breathed short and shallow.

"Hands up." It was Delgado's voice from above. "Both of your asses are under arrest."

Chen's stomach and heart took turns doing backflips. Her face went flush as relief washed over her. She flung the door open. "Iris," she called out and bounded up the stairs. There wasn't time to question how she knew to come here. It didn't matter—she was partnered up. They could handle this together. "How the hell did you find us?"

Delgado turned to look over at Chen. She cracked a smile. "I was wond…"

BOOM.

The bullet impacted Delgado's right temple, the bone and skin caved in. It burst from the other side of her head—the velocity and force shattering the majority of the left side of her skull and face—grey matter, bone, and blood sent on a trip across the room. The red crater left behind sizzled and smoked. The tight bun she kept her hair in was undone thanks to the force of impact. Hair slowly unraveled and fell over some of her face. Delgado dropped her gun—her good eye still locked on Chen. Her lips moved, but no sound came. She dropped to her knees, leaned to the left, and fell over. A single, long croak—and Delgado was gone.

Chen dropped the tire iron in her hand and screamed.

09

BLACKY'S EARS RANG. He saw Osito—gun in hand—the custom Sig Blacky loved so much. The report of the pistol a memory, he didn't bother to see what damage had been done to the officer only moments ago threatening them. He reached out with his left hand and took Osito's wrist, pushing the gun away from them. A flurry of punches with his right followed. Hitting Osito was like hitting a concrete wall, but Blacky ignored the immediate pain that shot from knuckle to wrist to elbow. Those punches rained down until he burdened Osito enough to force him to the ground.

"Oh my god, Iris, no—oh god." Blacky heard Chen behind him. After so many years—he knew it better than a favorite song.

A wave of guilt washed over Blacky. He did his best

to ignore it—concentrated on putting Osito down long enough to disarm him. No small feat—the little bear was still putting up a fight. Blacky managed to get his grip to loosen on the Sig. He batted it away and continued to pound at Osito's face. Osito smiled up to him—blood covered his nose and mouth. He spit at Blacky—sent every Spanish curse his way. There was laughter in his voice—a childish happiness. Blacky kept at it and finally, Osito went slack. The bastard wasn't dead, but Blacky figured there was enough blunt force trauma to keep him out of the game for a while.

Blacky rolled off of Osito. Sat down next to him and wiped his brow. Looked up in time to see one of the assholes that tagged him at the car customizing shop. Kid had the Sig in his hand and a smile on his face. "Do it," Blacky growled. He locked eyes with the piece of shit. No way would he give the prick any satisfaction of begging.

The kid didn't get a chance to respond with words or bullets. A volley tore into his midsection—extra-large holes ventilated his white tee-shirt. His body hit the floor in a shivering heap. Ahead, the second of Blacky's kidnappers bounded down the stairs. He was also greeted with a hail of gunfire. He was less fortunate than his partner. Most of the bullets caught his legs. He collapsed screaming and holding his left knee—the bone showing through his ruined jeans.

"Danny, get up. Hands behind your head," there

was a tremor in her voice. Agent Chen moved over to Blacky. Aimed Delgado's Glock down at him.

Blacky sighed. "Good to see you too." Looked up at her. "How long's it been?" He examined his boots. The pain in his face was alive now. Every beat of his heart seemed to echo across his face and inside his head.

Chen pressed the gun against his crown. "Stand up—now." There was the threat of tears in her voice—she was on the edge of losing it. "We're done here. You're under arrest."

"Whatever you want." He raised his hands and stood up. "Was that your partner?"

Chen stayed silent. Held the gun up. Blacky knew he struck a nerve—she pressed it a little harder against his head.

"No handcuffs then?" Blacky looked around the room. A dead body, two severely injured gentlemen, an unconscious, potentially handicapped Osito, and a groaning Junkie at the bottom of the stairs to his right. He pointed to them, then jabbed a thumb at Osito. "Think you should worry about these scumbags."

"I'm worried about keeping this insanity from spreading any further." Chen clenched her teeth. Wiped an eye with a free hand.

There were more noises upstairs—footsteps and what sounded like furniture being dragged along the floor. Blacky stared at the ceiling. "What if there's more thugs?"

Chen answered with a knee to Blacky's groin.

Blacky keeled over. "Fucker…" He took a few deep breaths. "Aside from our professional matters, Lindy—you seem to forget you were the one left me standing with my dick in the wind."

"No history. This bullshit got my friend…" Chen paused. Her eyes went glassy.

More noise upstairs—a scream.

"Fuck's sake, let me go upstairs. Ain't no exit—worse that can happen is I catch a few bullets. Make your job easier."

"There's no reason to let you do that." She narrowed her eyes.

Blacky pointed to Osito and down the stairs. "You got the gun." He looked to Delgado's body. "Unless your friend's killer is better to you a free man."

Her eyes darted to the side—it was how he knew she was thinking. Chen lowered the Glock. She deflated. "Fine. Go."

Blacky ran to the stairs leading to the second floor. "Keep eyes open. Son of a bitch is made of stone."

"Don't tell me how to do my job. Just get upstairs—you've got five minutes before I follow you up and shoot you—that's not a threat."

He went up the steps. Stopped halfway up and frowned. "Whatever it means to you, Lindy—I'm sorry about your friend. This was a private matter."

Chen turned and jabbed a finger at him—fury in

her eyes. "That you turned into another circus like you always do. This was the kind of bullshit that was never compatible with mine." She waved him away. "Four minutes, now."

"I get it. Again—apologies." Blacky continued upstairs. Felt ice in his gut. She was right—he'd sooner die than admit it—but she was.

"Worry about it after I throw you in a cell to rot." She waved her gun at his back.

Blacky stepped out onto the second floor landing. He leaned a hand against the fake wood grain paneling lining the walls. The wall felt sticky. He pulled the hand away for fear of why it would be in that state. To his right was a long hall—two doors each at either side, a window at the end. The window was boarded up with plywood. There was marker graffiti all over the board—a list of visitors to Osito's domicile. Dim ensconced lamps gave only enough light to confirm nobody waited in the shadows. Blacky let out a shrill whistle. No response. He walked over to the first door on his left, leaned his back against the wall, and gently knocked against the doorframe. "Hello?"

The sound of movement was the only response. Seemed panicked—like an animal.

For a moment, Blacky wondered if Osito was crazy enough to actually own a bear. Would he have to fight a bear? That would be a story no one would believe. For the safety of his body and his reputation, Blacky said a silent Hail Mary in the hopes that a forest-dwelling carnivore was not in the room. He reached forward and grabbed the door handle. Turned it—not locked. Blacky jerked the door open and laid his back flat—hesitant to step past the threshold in case a shotgun—or bear—were waiting. After a solid minute of silence, he found a little bravery and stepped into the room. It was dark. He reached to his right and found a light switch. Flicked it up and the room was bathed in light. Blacky's eyes widened at the scene before him. "Jesus fucking wept."

10

"**I SHOULD HAVE SHOT HIM,**" Chen muttered to herself. She rested Delgado's gun against her forehead—wandered the room and opened all the windows. She even opened the front door. The block was silent. Not even birds were calling, even though the sun was still out. No sirens in the distance—no backup. Something went wrong. Chen didn't want to be negative, but the wait had been too long. Her mind started to rush with ideas; maybe the cops in the area were on the take or maybe the 911 dispatcher was lying to her. Why would a dispatcher lie to her? Chen placed a hand over her heart—took long, slow breaths. She told herself not to be typical. There was training—time spent to avoid panic. She squeezed the grip of Delgado's pistol as hard as she could and settled down. No back up? Fine. She'd sort this mess out on her own—her terms.

The thug she tagged in the legs sluggishly rolled onto his back. He stared at the wall, face pale and eyes empty. The pool of blood below him was still wet and expanded—he was bleeding out. Chen watched him a moment. Caught herself wondering if scum like that was better off dying. They made life hell for so many— why not let him die? She shook the thoughts away. There was a reason she became a special agent. Her days of selfish free-wheeling were long gone. Chen brought her phone out of her pocket and dialed 911 again. Got a fast busy signal. Looked at the screen— no signal. "Holy shit, fuck these phones—really, fuck these phones." Chen was convinced she was cursed at this point.

"You having trouble?" The voice was familiar.

Chen turned. Junkie woke up. His eyes were red— blood gummed up his nostrils. His right eye had grown a little mouse underneath it. Chen guessed it was from his fall. She raised Delgado's gun. "Stay put." Stepped back a few paces. Wouldn't help her accuracy, but she couldn't stand to be near the piece of trash.

Junkie raised Blacky's Sig and grinned. "Who you think is quicker, baby?" He looked over to the uncon- scious Osito and Big Man. Eyed the dead and dying members of his clique. His jaw clenched. "Look at this shit. Ya'll messed up my boys bad." Junkie pointed at his bloodied face. "All ya'll gonna pay for this shit." He scanned the room. "Where the Elvis dude go?"

Chen stood steady. "This is my job. Put the weapon down and maybe we work something out. There's backup on the way and I don't think you'd enjoy the time assaulting a federal officer will earn you."

Junkie shook his head. "Don't try to turn this around. You motherfuckers poked your heads in the wrong spot. Gotta learn we own these fucking streets."

They watched each other for what felt like eons. She heard her breath and heartbeat inside of her head. Felt like her hands were trembling, but couldn't tell it by sight. The details around her seemed more vivid—the reds were brighter, the smells more crisp. She noticed the how dirty her hands were, but couldn't remember how they got that way. Junkie seemed to almost glow. He was covered in sweat and blood. It ran in faded trails down his chin and arms—his track marks providing a little direction.

A single moment. A breath. They were the center of each other's universe.

They pulled their triggers.

Both guns let out a 'click' instead of the expected death sentence.

Chen almost laughed as her world become banal again.

The Junkie eyed the Sig, confused. He pulled the

trigger a few more times—as if the gun was lying to him about being empty.

Chen took the opportunity from the distraction. Closed the distance between them and swung at his idiot face as hard as she could with bottom of the gun's grip. Junkie was quicker than she anticipated. He leaned back and took a glancing blow to the chin. That woke him up—he roared and tackled Chen. Ran her into the wall and shook the gun out of her hand. Chen drove an elbow into his back—once, twice, three times. Junkie was strong. He pulled her away from the wall and drove her into it again—forced all the air right out of her. Her legs wobbled, but she found the will to push back—to drive a heel into the toe of his Converse.

Junkie stepped back. Grabbed Chen by the hair and yanked her to the side. She let out a yelp, but grabbed at the arm holding onto her with both hands. Dug her nails into the track marks and drew blood. Swung her foot into his crotch as hard as she could. Junkie hic-cupped, lost his legs a moment, and let go of her hair. Chen wound up and delivered a vicious uppercut to Junkie's midsection. He gasped and dropped to his knees—cupped his aching privates and groaned like an old dog.

Chen's temper flared. The past few hours caught up with her and the Junkie was there—right now. He was a part of this. He was one of the people who made this happen. She felt fire rush up her chest and into her face. Her eyes felt white hot and wet. "Motherfucker." Chen grabbed Junkie by the head and pulled his face into her rising knee. Ignored the snaps and cracks she heard and repeated the motion—alternated her knees over and over. Her legs burned, her lungs struggled to keep up with her. Each strike left a growing bloom of crimson on her pants. The rhythm came easy—like marching. Even the noise of her knees against his face toned down to wet slaps. Junkie went limp, but she kept at it. In her mind, she was doing this to Blacky, to Osito—even Special Agent in Charge McAllister. She was seeking closure for the hell that came to her door that morning over a god damn car. She let out a roar and let go. Junkie fell over and laid still. He wasn't breathing anymore.

Beside them, the thug with the shot up legs let out a slow hiss of air, twitched, and closed his eyes for the last time.

Chen broke down. Sobbed uncontrollably. Her legs gave up on her and she fell to her knees. Her hands shook so severely even she thought it was comical. Chen ignored the pain shooting up and down from her hips to her knees. She covered her face with her trembling hands. "I'm so sorry Iris…I'm so sorry." Draped herself over the cooling body of Iris Delgado. "I'm so sorry."

11

THE ROOM SMELLED STRANGE; like ammonia and cooking meat—it burned Blacky's nose and eyes. The heat seemed to favor the entire floor, but the rooms could easily have been another five degrees warmer. The floor was littered with refuse. Clothes, old boxes of cereal, used condom wrappers, and various household items were everywhere. In some spots the garbage seemed to make the room smaller. He spotted a large bucket on wheels in the corner of the room—the kind a school janitor would use. The nuclear holocaust state of the room didn't interest Blacky, though. What really interested him were the six girls huddled in the corner near the radiator next to a sealed window.

He blinked—astonished and for the first time in a long time—at a loss for words.

One of the girls—the oldest—broke the silence. Her words were a hyper sing-song of what sounded to be Spanish, but Blacky couldn't make sense of it. The rhythm wasn't like the Nuyorican Spanglish he'd grown so used to in the five boroughs. She moved her arms wildly, pointed to the other girls and the window then the door. Her initially panicked tone gave way to something more aggressive. She was angry. Blacky didn't blame her.

He held a hand up. "Alright love, I can put two and two together. I need you to calm down." Blacky looked around the room. Struggled to recall any Spanish he may have picked up. "Uh, es mas ninas?"

The older girl nodded. She pointed out of the room towards the other doors.

"Very well." Blacky left the room. Walked to the door straight ahead. This one was locked. He grunted. Lifted a leg and brought his heel against the space between cheap door lock and the catch on the door frame. The wood buckled and the door opened towards him—whoever hung it was clearly an idiot. Blacky poked his head in and found a similar scene to the first room. The other two doors produced the same results—a group of young girls, buckets for bathrooms, and piles of garbage. He herded them all into a single room. Not a one of them spoke English, but he had a regular United Nations available. Polish,

Russian, Spanish, Portuguese—it seemed Osito had a hand in something far worse than hot cars.

The girls had the vacant stare of the freshly dead—none of the sparkly optimism you'd see in a young girl living a normal life to be found. Blacky felt his ears go hot. His neck itched. Kept his distance from the majority that seemed to be quick to distrust him. He figured they were right—he was no saint. Thankfully, he wasn't a monster either. "Girls—listen." He struggled to entertain a universal means of expressing help was on the way. Remembered how to say 'police' in all the languages he could muster. "*Policia, politsiya*, uh, *policja…gyeongchal*?" He pointed down at the floor.

Some of the girls got the gist of his message and spoke in hurried, hushed tones to one another. They were all so different, but dressed nearly the same—cheap shirts, shorts, no shoes, and no makeup. He wondered if this was the downtime appearance or if the sick sons of bitches that hired Osito's services preferred their exploitation to be as third-world authentic as possible. The thought of it had him seeing red.

Blacky ignored his impulses to run downstairs and brain Osito with a dumbbell. He instead did a quick headcount of the girls. 17.

17 of how many more? He cracked the knuckles of his fists and thought about how many had come in and out of this house. Wondered where they may have ended up. Were they alive? Saved by a gullible sugar

daddy who decided to be a white knight at the very last minute? No. He knew the answer to his question. Knew the fate of almost any of the girls thrust into this fresh hell. A chill ran down his back and he swallowed. Clenched his fists until his knuckles went white. Fuck the Plymouth, Osito had this horror to answer for.

He walked to the bedroom door and turned. "Pera aqui?" Blacky's gaze was on the older Spanish girl.

She nodded and communicated the message to others with words and hand gestures.

Blacky gave her a thin smile. He was glad that his Spanish was sufficient enough to keep things from getting out of hand. Last thing he needed was innocent blood shed because he wanted his car back. "I'll be back." He exited the room and strayed at the top of the stairs. Blacky held his hips and let his head hang. Exhaustion hit him like a brick to the forehead. The discovery of the girls was icing on a turd. There were other matters. He needed to sort things with Chen—as much as he'd rather not look at her. That would come last. First, Osito—son of a bitch was due worse than a simple beating. Blacky decided that severe brain damage was a perfectly viable option.

It always came back to crippling idiots. Tony was right—Blacky might have had a violence problem. He made a mental note to buy something nice for Tony if this mess sorted itself out tidily. If not, the lack of Blacky in any of their lives would be gift enough.

Downstairs, someone was talking. Something went bump. Something shattered. Chen screamed.

Blacky bounded down the stairs. Stopped dead when he was greeted with the sight of Chen driving her knees into a thug's face. She muttered something with each strike—too low to tell what she was saying. He wanted to run over and pull her away—stop her before she went too far, but it was too late. Chen stopped driving her knees into the thug's pulverized face. Her grip released and he fell to the side—lifeless. Blacky didn't recognize his face, but assumed he wasn't a new guest to the party. Chen interrupted his flow of thought and sobbed like a baby on top of her partner's body. There was a time he would have run over to console her—to assure her none of this was on her head. That was too far from his character, though. There had been a time when he gave a shit about Linda Chen, but that time was long gone.

Besides, he didn't particularly need Chen turning all that anger on him.

12

CHEN SNIFFED AND WIPED HER EYES. She realized this was
too vulnerable a position to be in and worked to regain
her composure—there was still so much work to do.
She stood up—shakily. Didn't notice Blacky at the foot
of the stairs.

She blinked when she finally saw him. "How long
have you been there?"

His face was blank. "I let you have at it—figured you
could do with the anger release." Blacky scratched the
back of his neck and stared at Junkie. "Though, we got
bigger problems." He stepped downstairs and picked
his Sig up from the floor. Slipped it into his waist band.

Chen watched him. "Hey, you don't need a…"

Blacky raised a hand. "It ain't loaded."

Chen felt her face flush. "I swear to God, Danny…"

"Fine." He pulled the piece back out, laid it at his feet and kicked it over. "Jesus, you keep calling me that." Blacky examined the bodies of the dead. Rifled through their pockets. "Been at least three dogs' ages since I last heard anyone say that name."

"It's your name." Chen watched him scavenge. "Why are you going through their pockets? It's disgusting."

"I don't disagree, Lindy. It's an undignified thing to do, but…" He didn't look up at her or stop what he was doing. "…what dignity these men had died a long fucking time ago." Blacky stood up. "Besides, nothing doing. No parting gifts for any of us."

They stood in silence. Blacky looked out the open front door. "No back up yet?"

"No…I'm getting worried."

"Well, it's worse." Blacky pointed upstairs. "Seventeen girls. None older than fifteen."

Chen's gaze followed his finger. She looked up to the darkness at the top of the stairs. "Bullshit." No way was she going to let Blacky distract her this way. No way that the situation could be worse. In her mind there was no worse. This was as bad as it could have gone.

Blacky rubbed his temples. "I've got no time to quarrel with you. Believe me or not, this entire mess got bigger than any one of us—especially my fucking Polly." He looked over to the weight benches. His eyes widened. "Where's Osito?"

Osito was gone. Only a bloodstain on the carpet hinted he had been laid out minutes ago.

Chen looked around the room. "Jesus." She hadn't seen him move, but there was no way to be sure. Her fight with the junkie was a blur—all noise. For all she knew, the attack had been a way to let Osito get away.

Blacky groaned. "Shit…"

The roar of an engine came from downstairs—the Fury.

"Shit, shit, shit." Blacky ran to the front door. "This miserable son of a bitch has got the fucking balls to take my car again."

Chen followed. Peeked over Blacky's shoulders and watched the '59 Plymouth Fury peel out down the block. Osito's head barely cleared the steering wheel. There was a smile on his face.

Blacky turned and held a hand out. "Your car keys."

"What?" Chen widened her eyes. "I can't let you go. You're still under arrest."

Blacky shook his head. "The son of a bitch needs catching right, or do you find yourself okay with this pint-sized fucker getting away?" He grabbed Chen by the shoulder. "He needs to pay for what he did to your partner and the girls up there. Your way won't cut it." Blacky was dead serious. His jaw was granite set.

She didn't want to admit it, but he was right. "Again with this my way or your way garbage…" She stopped herself. No time for bullshit arguments about the past. Chen shook her head. "I don't even have my keys."

"Fine, fuck it." Blacky spread his arms out and leaned against the doorframe. Nodded to himself. "I got something." He took off at a sprint and bounded down the stairs. "Go upstairs. Look for yourself. Help those girls." He turned and smiled. "Don't think we'll be seeing one another again, so take care."

She watched him disappear. There was the smallest probability she'd be able to track him down again, but Blacky was right. If he lived through this—if he got his hands on Osito—he'd be a phantom. It would be another two years before she'd even get a whisper of him. "Crap," she muttered. Turned on a heel. Tried to ignore the bloodbath at her feet. Chen marched to the stairs, climbed up slowly. "Hello?"

She heard hushed voices.

Chen paused midway up. Cocked her head towards the open front door—sirens. A wave of relief washed over. "Thank God, finally." She jogged up the remaining steps. "Hello? This is special agent Linda Chen. I'm here to help." A part of her wondered if she was talking to thin air. She wouldn't put it past Blacky to fuck with her head—mix her up to make an escape after he had dealt with Osito.

There was an open bedroom door bleeding light into the dark hallway. Chen walked in. Saw Blacky wasn't lying. The smell of the place hit her like a fist.

The girls eyed her suspiciously. A few whispered to each other—voices filled with an urgent fear and doubt.

"Hi." Chen forced a smile. She reached into her back pocket—empty. She sighed. Forgot Big Man probably still had her wallet and badge. She raised a finger. "One second, okay?" She ran back downstairs. Big Man had moved himself under a window and was seated with his back against the wall. He looked as if he was crying blood. Chen couldn't tell if he was asleep. She walked up to him and poked his flank with the tip of her toe. "Asshole."

Big Man's neck snapped towards the sound of her voice. He licked his lips. "I need help. Please."

Chen didn't feel bad. "Help's on the way. Where's my badge?"

He looked confused. Looked away from her a moment. He reached into his pants pocket and procured her wallet. "You the Fed?"

"I said *my* wallet, right?" She snatched it away and turned to head back upstairs.

"I'm sorry." Big Man called out. "Osito…he ain't the type you say no to."

"Something tells me saying yes to him isn't worth it either. Stay put. There should be people coming soon." Chen double-timed it back upstairs. Held the badge high as she entered the bedroom and the girls responded with a rush of enthusiasm. Chen managed to herd them all downstairs. Ushered them as far away from the bloody chaos as possible. This meant all of those poor girls were stuck out on the front stoop. Chen ensured they stayed put and wandered back inside. The sirens now sounded loud enough to be heard down the street. Chen's phone vibrated in her pocket—a local number. She connected. "Linda Chen."

"Chen?" The voice belonged to her supervisor—Eric Macallister. "What the fuck is going on over there? Do you have Clarke in custody?" Son of a bitch didn't bother to ask if she was alright.

Chen didn't care. For the first time during her exile at the Queens remote office, she was happy to hear his stupid voice. She rubbed her eyes and took off her suit jacket. Draped it over Delgado's body. The jacket hit the floor with a hard thud near the pocket. Chen cocked her head to the side and dug into it. Found the keys to the Mazda she pocketed earlier. "Ah…yeah…" She stood up. "Sorry, Danny," she whispered.

13

BLACKY MANAGED TO HOTWIRE an Accord in record time. He drove the car down Fteley Avenue and made a wide turn onto the Metcalf Avenue. Figured Osito didn't have a monumental lead on him—with some fast driving, he could catch up. He wagered a guy like this had to have other houses in the area with as many or more girls. Osito wasn't a genius, but he had an enterprise. A guy with an ego five times his size wouldn't just run away and drop off the radar—he'd check in on other spots, get his underlings to hold the fort while he kept his head low. What he didn't count on was Osito being dumb enough to jump on the Cross Bronx South, during rush hour, on a Friday.

Osito did exactly that—the absolutely dumbest thing he could have thought to do.

Blacky stopped the car short. He could see his Plymouth a quarter mile off on the opposite side of the highway. "What a fucking wanker," he told himself with a smile. Blacky followed the Cross Bronx up to Watson Avenue, hung a left and then hung another left onto Morrison Avenue. He dumped the car on the corner and ran the rest of the way down the entrance ramp to the highway. The Plymouth moved a few hundred yards, but it was still visible. Blacky stared at the back of Osito's head as he strut between the middle and right lanes. The occasional honk followed him. He flipped those drivers off. Gave them each a custom sneer. On the opposite side of the highway, cars and trucks moved along at a steady clip. Blacky could only assume there was an accident close to the George Washington Bridge.

He wasn't surprised.

The Cross Bronx Expressway was one of the most notoriously congested and dangerous roads in America. Blacky was out to make the latter point something Osito would learn personally. He let himself dwell on the state of those girls—on the state of their clothes and the rooms they were locked in. Like sheep or cattle. Waiting for the piper to come calling. He wondered if it would be worth tapping Chen to feed him any potential information found on clients. He'd have a full Christmas list of bastards with skulls that needed cracking over the holidays.

Osito was busy honking his horn and cursing at anyone who could hear him. The Fury's top was down. Blacky smiled to himself—mistake number two. He stepped up his pace. Licked his lips. He had gooseflesh he wanted to get his hands on this bastard so bad. The car—whatever—it didn't matter anymore. So long as Blacky was concerned, he owed Osito as much misery as he could deliver for each and every man, woman, and child he had exploited in the name of dirty profit.

Blacky broke into a short sprint. "Baby bear!" He leapt forward, cupped the back Osito's head with his right hand, and drove the prick's face into the steering wheel with all his might. Osito's head snapped back—a handful of gashes from the prior beating immediately reopened and bled anew. He grunted, dazed from the surprise attack. Blacky lifted Osito from the driver's seat by the neck and flung him against the Camry unfortunate enough to be idle next to them. The driver—a young professional—flinched and did his best to ignore the fracas.

Osito leaned against the Camry. Shook the bats out of his head. He straightened up and spit at Blacky's feet. "I was hoping this shit wasn't over between us. Was gonna find your ass one way or another. Get one of my dudes in Riker's to gank you—or maybe wait and do it my fucking self."

Blacky raised his fists. "That why you took Polly

with you? Got a crush on me? Give me a reason to come find you if I made it out?"

Osito matched Blacky's stance and smiled. "We animals, right? Got us a shared interest and shit."

"I found the girls, Osito." Blacky's mood darkened. He took a step to the left.

Osito took a step to the right. His face was stone—nothing to read. "That's a damn shame."

"Cops are probably headed there right now."

Osito shook his head. "Ah, see, that made your problems a lot worse."

They began circling each other like they did at the house. Each man feinting forward momentum—waiting to see who would make the first move. Horns sounded off, but traffic was still in the same spot. Blacky wondered if it was actually fanfare—some encouragement to beat Osito's ass into the asphalt. His impatience got the best of him. "Fuck it." Blacky darted forward, felt Osito out with a quick jab-hook combination.

Osito took the first hit clean. Smiled. "You hit like a pansy ass motherfucker." Osito emulated Blacky's actions. Jab, jab, hook.

Blacky backed away. He watched all three punches miss their target. "You're talking big now. Like you weren't asleep like a toddler before." He moved in again. Pushed Osito against the Camry for another go and launched alternating punches to the ribs. He counted off in his head, 'one-two-three-four'—a mantra to help keep the rhythm.

Osito tucked his elbows in. Pulled away from Blacky's punches like a pro. The hits connected, but he didn't seem fazed. If anything, the punches seemed to ramp him up. His smile was steady, his eyes were bright. Osito pushed Blacky back and lay in with his own body blows.

Blacky was caught off guard. Some of the punches came in lower than he expected. Osito laid in closer to the groin, peppered in a few near the kidneys—this was a street fight, rules didn't matter. Blacky had to remind himself of that. He lifted a boot and kicked forward as hard as he could. He connected with Osito's midsection and sent him sprawling over the hood of the Camry and to the opposite side of the car. The Camry's owner continued to gawk. Blacky wasted no time. He rushed over to Osito and swung a hammer punch to the back of the head. Osito dodged the brunt of it. Blacky paid with an uppercut to the jaw that got his head ringing.

Osito came in. Grabbed Blacky by the collar and yanked him down to eye level. "Got your ass now." He drove his head into Blacky's broken nose.

The pain was intense—like a knife slipping into the center of his face and into the corners of his eyes. The world spun around and his eyes crossed. He felt more blows to his face and midsection. The next moment he felt the hot asphalt on his face and Osito was bringing his boots down on his head. Blacky ignored the signs of permanent damage and reached his hands out. He tried to grab at Osito's foot—missed the mark the first three attempts, but nailed the fourth. Blacky pulled as hard as he could. Brought Osito's leg over his shoulder and willed himself to stand. Osito was heavy. Blacky stood to full height, Osito's head a foot off the ground. He brought his arms up, gave Osito a little more height, and let go.

Osito fell face first on the road. His neck twisted before the rest of his body caught up with him. He let out an 'oomph'. Laid still for a moment.

Blacky stumbled over to the median that separated the north and south sides of the highway. He leaned his lower back against the concrete. Brought a hand to his nose slowly—fearful of what he'd feel. His fingers brushed over what was surely an open gash. He recoiled at his own touch. "Fucking hell."

Osito was on his hands and knees. He panted. Started laughing. "We some fucked up dudes, huh?"

Blacky nodded. He heard sirens close by. "We can always beat feet. Set up an appointment for another time and finish it all like proper gentlemen."

"Ain't no next time." Osito struggled to his feet. He was in a bad state, but Blacky didn't have a mirror to compare their wounds. Osito's face was puffy and cut up all over. His left hand was pulled up close to his chest. When he stepped forward, there was a hint of a limp.

Blacky felt pleased to know that if this ended in death or arrest—he got a few damn good licks in. He straightened himself out. "You know, originally, I was just gonna kick your ass."

Osito snorted. Choked back a laugh.

Blacky narrowed his eyes. Something obstructed the view from his left side. He assumed that was on account of the swelling. "Then I found what you had going upstairs." He looked towards the onramp. Traffic left the police on the avenue. None of them had the common sense to get the fuck out of their cars.

"So what? I got a fucking empire to worry about." Osito raised his good arm and motioned to the cars as if they were his subjects. "You gonna hate on a dude for thinking big?"

"Fuck right off with your bullshit Scarface fantasies." Blacky spit. Pointed a finger. "You're an inadequate prick that took all that hostility and resentment and turned into a fucking bully." He pointed the at himself. "Me? I'm a fucking scoundrel, but at least I'm not pussy enough to fuck with kids. I fight in my weight rank..." He grinned. "Short-Round."

That got Osito's goat. He grit his teeth and came at Blacky with renewed vigor.

Blacky had an edge—two good hands and no limp. He grabbed Osito by the neck and spun him around—got a few punches in while he did it. With Osito's back to the median, Blacky leaned him over. A passing car let out a wail that traveled down the distance of the north side of the highway as it flew by. Osito looked at the oncoming traffic with panic in his eyes.

"Yo, don't get crazy." He grabbed at Blacky with one good hand.

"I ain't a fucking homicidal maniac." Blacky turned his head to watch the oncoming traffic on the other side of the median. He playfully shoved Osito enough to give him another scare and cackled. "Relax, relax. Only punctuating the sentence a little." Black wrapped Osito's silver cross and chain around his hand. Yanked it free.

Osito flinched and raised his hands up in surrender. "Point made." There wasn't fear in his eyes anymore.

Blacky smelled a rat. He chewed on the inside of his cheek. Clicked his tongue against his teeth. "Nah, fuck it." Blacky kicked Osito dead center in the chest as hard as he could. Sent the bastard tumbling over the median.

Osito scrambled to his feet despite his wounds. Stood up in time to catch sight of the oncoming 18-Wheeler. It slammed into him at near full speed. The brakes engaged too late and he became a hundred yard stain on the Cross Bronx Expressway. Blacky shook his head. "I ain't beyond a little old-fashioned revenge." The truck skidded to a halt. Blacky eyed the red smear detailing Osito's last trip in the Bronx. He lifted Osito's silver cross to eye level and slipped it off the silver rope chain—tossed the cross out into the oncoming traffic across the way. "The chain's nicer." He clasped it around his neck. "Besides, I ain't a god-fearing man."

Traffic started to move again on his side of the highway, so Blacky made a break for the Fury. It sat in wait; the engine purring. He hopped in, shifted the car into drive, and swerved through traffic like a madman. After passing a few exits, he spotted the cigarette hole in the Fury's passenger seat and frowned.

He poked a finger into the hole. "Son of a bitch really did deserve to die."

The cops and their fancy lights finally appeared in his rear view mirror. Blacky spot checked his location—smiled. It was only a few more miles to the city.

14

"CAN WE GO ANY FASTER?" Chen leaned on the dash of the police cruiser. She flagged down the first cop she saw and hitched a ride. Had to flash her badge and swing her dick around—figuratively—to convince him to do her the solid.

The officer tasked to drive her frowned. "The suspect's driving a nineteen fifty-nine Plymouth, Agent Chen. We won't lose him."

Chen gave a bitter laugh. "Sorry, with everything that's gone wrong today, I wouldn't be surprised if he up and flies away." She searched the console by the window sill. "How do you roll down the window?"

The officer ignored her.

The Fury was in sight for most of the pursuit. Chen noted that while Blacky kept ahead of them; he didn't seem to be in much of a rush to lose them. That didn't feel right—Blacky was seasoned. The man knew how to shake off about anyone in most situations. There was a time she considered him a greasy ghost. She tied her hair back and wondered what the hell he was up to.

The radio in the cruiser chirped. "Please be advised, EMT requested to Cross Bronx north. Second suspect is down. Truck involved in accident."

Chen furrowed her brow. That had to be Osito. She almost smiled. The son of a bitch was dead—good. Normally she wouldn't revel in that kind of thinking, but she took solace in the fact that everyone was allowed at least one 'cheat' day. She could afford a momentary lapse of moral judgement.

The Fury pulled off the highway at the last stop— headed towards the Henry Hudson. They continued to follow, although slowed down because of the sudden change in road width. Blacky went southbound. The road opened back up and soon enough, they were only a few car lengths behind him. Blacky sped up and led them to the 95th Street exit. He broke a few more laws and parked his car right by Riverside Park, exited the vehicle, and sprinted down a rickety pier.

Chen smacked the officer on the side of the arm. "Stop, stop, stop."

He rolled his eyes, pulled the cruiser over, and hit the brakes. Stared blankly at Chen.

"Tell the rest of them to stand down. I'll handle

this until my superior shows up." She ran out of the car—left the door open. Figured the officer could use another reason to hate her guts. Chen fished her badge from her pocket and held it up as she ran to inform the other cruisers pulling up that she was legitimate, also, to not get shot. "Hold back!" she screamed multiple times.

Blacky stood at the end of the pier facing her. He smirked and tipped an invisible hat. His face was swollen and covered in blood—shoulders were slack and his arms hung loose at his sides. Somehow, his hair was still in place. The exhaustion was apparent in his eyes. Chen thought he looked as if he really did go toe to toe with a bear. Maybe this was one big production leading to surrender. There was nowhere left for Blacky to go. Last she knew, he couldn't swim. Even if he could, with state he was in, Chen gave him less than 50 yards before the Hudson ate him alive.

Chen pulled Delgado's Glock from her waistband. "Hands up." She rested her thumb on the back of the pistol grip, her index finger hovered over the trigger. "Can't believe how many times I've had to tell you that today, Danny."

Blacky lifted his arms—winced as he did so. "How are the girls?"

Chen tried to hide her surprise at the question. Tucked her chin into her chest as she aimed down sight. "They're fine. All on the way to the hospital to get help." She swallowed. "I'm sorry I didn't believe you about that."

Blacky laughed. "Don't blame you. I'd've thought I was trying to weasel my way out of a bad situation with that line too." He looked past her. "Your friends look ready to Butch and Sundance me."

Chen turned her head back quickly. A good precinct's worth of angry cops were out and aiming their service pistols at Blacky. She looked back to him. "You're a wanted man and there are a few things you have to answer for, Danny. Don't be so surprised you'd get this much attention." Chen pointed at the silver rope chain around Blacky's neck with her piece. "So, where'd you get the new jewelry?"

He locked his eyes back onto hers. "I killed him. Just so you know. The son of a bitch is road kill now. Imagine it'll take a while for the truck driver that him to get that grill shining again."

They watched each other.

Chen took a single step forward. "Why didn't you leave with me?" The question came out of her before she had a chance to stop it.

"I'm sorry, what?" He narrowed his eyes and frowned.

"When we met. You knew what I was—you knew why I was there." Chen kept her aim steady. "I would have left it all for you, if only you'd have stopped your bullshit."

Blacky scoffed. "Christ, Lindy. I wasn't about to go and fuck your life up any more than it already was." He looked down at his feet. "Besides, you didn't have much trouble leaving me behind and giving me up to your handlers."

"You went to Northern Ireland either way." She was louder now. "I saw what you did in the papers—to that man in Newry."

Blacky looked down a moment. A flicker of recognition came to life in his eyes. "John Collins… Jesus. Haven't thought of that in a long, long time." He sighed. "If it means anything to you, Lindy, I wasn't the one that killed that man. I mean, yes, I was there for it, but my hands didn't shed the blood on that one."

The uncomfortable silence came back with a vengeance. Chen with her gun aimed at his chest and Blacky looking off into the distance.

"Are you going to come in with me?" Chen tried to add an edge to her voice, but failed.

Blacky seemed to grow an inch. His eyes sparkled and he smiled the way she remembered him smiling in the better days. "What's the fun in that?" He raised a hand to the police behind her. "Just emptying my pockets officers," he called out. Blacky tossed his keys at Chen's feet. "Take her. Someone needs to take good care of her." He took two steps back to the edge of the pier.

Chen stepped forward. "Danny, don't you dare."

He took another step back—anymore and he'd be off the pier and into the water. A tugboat was passing by, making its presence known with the sounding of its foghorn. Chen lost her focus for a split second, distracted by the noise. That was when Blacky let himself fall backwards. She froze, at a loss for what to do. It wasn't as if she could shoot him back on to the pier.

Blacky fell into the Hudson with a splash. Chen ran to the edge of the pier and scanned the ebbing surface of the brackish water. It was broad daylight, but she couldn't see a damn thing. She turned on a heel and waved over to the police. She spotted Macallister behind an undercover vehicle—his scowl visible from a quarter mile away.

• • •

Three hours later and nothing. No sign of a body or any calls from the Coast Guard. Either Blacky sunk like a stone to lay his final rest in the cold, dirty Hudson or he got away again.

"So, nothing, huh?" Special Agent Supervisor McAllister looked out at New Jersey—his scowl hadn't left his face in hours. Chen suspected it got stuck like that. She pegged him for the kind of man that never listened to his mother.

"Nothing." Chen reached into her back pocket. Offered her badge and Delgado's service piece to him.

"Guessing you want these. The pistol isn't mine—it's Delgado's." She near choked saying the name.

Macallister took both from her. "You're not in as much trouble as you think, but some time away from the job is advisable. Give yourself a week, and then we'll talk about what comes next. Keep yourself available in case anyone has extra questions." He placed a hand on her shoulder. "This thing with the girls you found, Linda. I don't think you realize how big this is. Shit, it's bigger than that idiot mick or the Puerto Rican street stain, I promise that."

She nodded. "Are they okay?"

Macallister finally smiled. "You and Iris got them out of that hellhole—yeah, I think they are."

"Good." She turned and walked towards the Fury. Opened the door and sat in the driver's seat. Swore she could smell him—even feel him. Chen started the car and it roared to life, eager to get on the road again.

"That's evidence, you know," Macallister said.

Chen smiled weakly. "We'll talk it over when I get back." She pulled out onto the road. Drove due south—decided to take the full circuit downtown and roll back up the FDR.

The Fury needed to stretch its legs.

15

"WHAT'LL YOU HAVE?" The waitress was heavy-set. Broad featured, and seemed to be in an ever present state of annoyance.

Blacky tapped his fingers on the red countertop and eyed the vintage menu above a row of cheap liquor. "All honesty, I have never had a, what do you call it again?"

"A ripper," she deadpanned.

"Alright, well, what's recommended?" He smiled. Hoped the state of the bruises and stitches on his face didn't evoke more of a negative reaction from his server.

"Well, you can have a ripper. Maybe some relish on it." She lazily pointed up. "We have burgers too."

Blacky scanned the menu items. Spotted fish and

chips. "Oh, smashing. Tell you what; let me get a ripper the way you said and an order of fish and chips. Pint of whatever lager you've got on tap too."

"You got it." She wandered off.

"This place smells like ass." Chen took a seat a single chair away from Blacky and on his left. She removed a pair of sunglasses and tucked them into her suit jacket. "This the kind of garbage you put inside of you while you're recuperating?"

The waitress walked back over with a pint of lager for Blacky. She eyed Chen. "What'll you have?" Her tone and delivery was exactly the same as before.

Blacky began to suspect their waitress was some kind of android.

"Just a burger—medium—and a coke, please." Chen smiled.

"Got it." The waitress wandered back off.

Blacky turned to Chen. 'So am I getting the time to enjoy my fried meal before you people drag me off?"

She laughed. "Nah, I'm still on paid leave. No arrests today. Besides, after everything that happened…" Chen shook her head, "…not too sure if I'll be sticking around to arrest your ass at all."

"Change of heart, then. Can't say I'm mad about that." He nodded to her. "Well, thanks for coming on out either way. Apologize for the whole…" he searched for the words. "…river thing."

"Yeah, sure. The 'river thing.'" Chen snatched a straw

from the dispenser in front of her and tore the wrapper from the top. She took the exposed tip and chewed on it nervously. "They're still going to come for you. Even out here in the lower north part of New Jersey."

He waved her away. "Ah, let them. I can always hide in the wilderness John Rambo style." He turned and looked out the window behind him. Saw the Plymouth sitting out front—freshly washed and waxed. "Taking good care of Polly, huh?"

"She's a fucking beast." Chen turned to look at the Fury as well. "Definitely see the appeal, though. Need to find someone to sort out the cigarette hole in the front passenger seat, though."

"I got a guy out in Queens that'll do it for a song if you mention my name." Blacky leaned his elbows on the countertop. "Remind me to give you his information."

"Is he in a wheelchair?" Chen arched a brow.

Blacky waved the remark away. "Nah, he's alright. Never inspired me to strike him."

The waitress came over with three plates. Placed two in front of Blacky and another in front of Chen. "Enjoy."

"Damn, that was fast." Blacky lifted a piece of fried fish to his mouth and took a massive bite. Ignored the burn and relished in the taste of fish, batter, and grease. "Been too fucking long."

Chen shook her head. "You are such a fucking

cliché." She pointed at his plate. "Fish and chips, starting fights—a fucking final standoff at a pier." She flipped him off. "Seriously, fuck you, Blacky Jaguar. You're such a drama queen. I preferred regular, old Danny Clarke."

Blacky shoved more fish in his mouth. Drained his beer and lifted the empty pint glass at the waitress. "Danny Clarke's long gone."

The waitress wandered over and snatched the empty pint glass away, came back with a full one.

"Thanks, love." Blacky looked back to Chen. "The ending was all a little bit of fun. If I was a betting man, I figured I wasn't seeing the next day, so what the hell? Decided to make it exciting for all of us." He picked up a fry and pointed it at Chen. "To change the subject. How are the girls?"

Chen frowned. "Most of them up and vanished from the hospital. The few who stayed are in a tough spot—better than before, mind you—but still tough. Turns out Osito had a few houses all over the Bronx with girls locked up inside. My boss says this is going to bust open one of the largest sex slave rings in New York history." She raised her Coke to him. "So kudos for that. Your irrational loyalty to a car and penchant for physical violence ended up helping a lot of people."

Blacky nodded. "And your partner's family?"

She looked away. Put her food back down. "I made

it five minutes into the burial. Didn't stick around to talk."

"I get it. Not easy to lose a partner and a friend." He shoved more fries into his mouth. Decided to take a chance on the ripper. It only took two bites to convince him. He motioned the waitress over. "Fucking hell, this is magnificent. Can you set me up with four more to take away?"

The waitress finally broke a smile and nodded. "Absolutely."

"Welcome to America. Danny." Chen gave his shoulder a gentle punch.

Blacky winced. "Fucking easy, I'm still tender." He took a pull from his pint glass. "Only fault of the place is I can't enjoy a cigarette." He jabbed a thumb towards the door. "You mind if I go and sneak a fag?"

"Go for it."

He slid off his stool. Tucked his hands into the pockets of his leather jacket. "By the way."

"Yeah?" Chen was busy with her fries now. Didn't look at him.

"Thanks again."

"For what?"

He rolled his eyes. Drained his new pint and motioned to the waitress for a refill. "You know damn well, what. I'll be back." Blacky walked outside, pulled a cigarette from his pocket, and lit it with a BIC.

There were a few grizzled, old bikers hanging out in

the parking lot smoking cigarettes and chatting it up about their bikes. They eyed Blacky for a moment and began to talk in hushed tones.

Blacky ignored them. Puffed away at his cigarette and inspected his face in the reflection of the window. He was looking a sight better than he was the week prior—even with the self-stitching. That had been a bit of a worry. He imagined he'd be left with fat, caterpillar-shaped scars. As if he wasn't cartoonish enough.

"Hey, Fonzie." The voice belonged to a lanky-looking son of a bitch in a fancy high-tech riding jacket and canvas chaps over his Levis.

Blacky watched him through the reflection of the window. Stayed quiet and finished his cigarette.

"You hear me, brother?" He walked over. Placed a hand on Blacky's shoulder.

A small jolt of pain ran through Blacky's shoulder and down his back. He turned slow. "Can I help you?"

The biker arched a brow. "Look funny and talk funny too, huh?"

Blacky narrowed his eyes. "Funny? You don't seem to be laughing much. Couldn't be that funny."

The biker smiled. Raised both hands up mockingly. "I'm wondering about that jacket of yours. That a vintage piece?" There was a vicious glint in his eyes—trouble. Blacky had seen it a million times before.

"It's a fine jacket indeed. Appreciate the compliment." He pushed his way past the biker and began to walk to the door. Unfortunately, the biker's friends decided to block that route off.

"Such a nice jacket, I was wondering if…"

"Fuck's sake, please let's not make this a complete a mess. Had enough messes the past few weeks. It's getting tired." Blacky rubbed his temples.

The bikers all looked at each other, confused.

Blacky turned around to face the 'leader'. He pulled his jacket off and tossed it at his feet. "Take it and fuck right off. No time to deal with this shit."

The biker stared at the jacket and sniffed. Hocked a loogie right on the snarling jaguar embroidered on the back. "You hand it to me like a fucking man."

Blacky smiled. "I choose not to."

A pair of hands gripped his shoulders. "Be smart and do as he says."

Blacky sighed. He bent at the waist and picked the jacket back up. Walked over to the head biker and held the jacket out. "Enjoy." His face was hot. Every single instinct screamed at him to strangle or hit the son of a bitch in front of him, but he thought about Chen's observation—about how he fell into these little traps and let himself be the caricature he thought himself to be. It actually gave him pause.

The biker took the jacket in hand. Inspected it and nodded to Blacky. He tossed it behind him like garbage. "Didn't realize it was the ladies' cut." He cackled.

His entourage laughed with him.

Blacky looked through the window of the diner. Watched Chen sucking at her soda and having a talk with the waitress. "You know what's really fucked? Not only is she right, but I couldn't even make it a single minute into a change of heart." Blacky grabbed the head biker by the back of the head and slammed it into the glass as hard as he could. A spiderweb of cracks emerged from the spot where the biker's head impacted. The waitress and Chen both turned—the former going slack-jawed while Chen rolled her eyes.

The head biker staggered back—a wet, red streak already running from forehead to the tip of his nose. He moaned and pawed at his face—fear in his moistening eyes.

Blacky turned, raised his fists, and cracked his neck. "Alright boys, I got a full belly and two pints in me. Let's scrap." He smiled like a mad man and came at the group with fists flying. Somewhere behind him, he heard Chen yelling at him to 'cut it out'. Blacky cackled and kept at it. This was his steady state—boiling blood, split knuckles, and new bruises.

Blacky Jaguar felt alive.

ACKNOWLEDGMENTS

First off, I'd like to thank my wife, Cheryl, and my kids, Logan, Dane, and Lula, for their patience with my obsessions and for being stalwart Giants fans. And to Ron Earl Phillips at Shotgun Honey Books for his tolerance of my haphazard approach to writing and for taking a chance on the book. Also, thanks to Joe Clifford and Bob Pitts for their insight and input. And lastly, thanks to Bryan Stow, whose tragic story was the impetus for this book.

ANGEL LUIS COLÓN is a Derringer Award and Anthony Award-nominated author writer of *HELL CHOSE ME*, the Blacky Jaguar novella series, *NO HAPPY ENDINGS*, and the short story collection *MEAT CITY ON FIRE AND OTHER ASSORTED DEBACLES*.

INFESTED (MTV Books/Simon & Schuster) is his debut YA novel.

ABOUT
SHOTGUN HONEY BOOKS

Thank you for reading *The Fury of Blacky Jaguar* by Angel Luis Colón.

Shotgun Honey began as a crime genre flash fiction webzine in 2011 created as a venue for new and established writers to experiment in the confines of a mere 700 words. More than a decade later, Shotgun Honey still challenges writers with that storytelling task, but also provides opportunities to expand beyond through our book imprint and has since published anthologies, collections, novellas and novels by new and emerging authors.

We hope you have enjoyed this book. That you will share your experience, review and rate this title positively on your favorite book review sites and with your social media family and friends.

Visit ShotgunHoneyBooks.com

SHOTGUN HONEY
FICTION WITH A KICK

www.ingramcontent.com/pod-product-compliance
Lightning Source LLC
Chambersburg PA
CBHW010558170726
48285CB00011B/2969